KISS ME, DEADLY

G·K Hall &Co.

Also published in Large Print
from G.K. Hall by Mickey Spillane:

The Killing Man
Twisted Thing

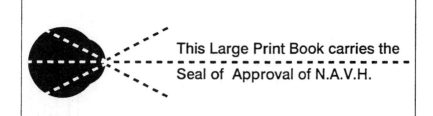

This Large Print Book carries the
Seal of Approval of N.A.V.H.

Kiss Me, Deadly

MICKEY SPILLANE

G.K. Hall & Co.
Thorndike, Maine

Published in Large Print by arrangement with Dutton, an imprint of New American Library, a division of Penguin Books USA Inc.

G.K. Hall Large Print Book Series.

Set in 16 pt. News Plantin by Melissa Harvey.

Printed on acid free paper in the United States of America.

Library of Congress Cataloging-in-Publication Data

Spillane, Mickey, 1918–
    Kiss me, deadly / by Mickey Spillane.
      p. cm.
    ISBN 0-8161-5554-2 (alk. paper : lg. print)
    ISBN 0-8161-5555-0 (alk. paper : lg. print : pbk)
    1. Hammer, Mike (Fictitious character — Fiction. 2. Private investigators — United States — Fiction. 3. Large type books.
I. Title.
[PS3537.P652K55 1993]
813'.52—dc20

                             93-4067
                               CIP

All characters and events
portrayed in this story are
fictitious. Any similarity
to persons living or dead
is purely coincidental.

M.S.

Chapter One

All I saw was the dame standing there in the glare
of the headlights waving her arms like a huge pup-
pet and the curse I spit out filled the car and my
own ears. I wrenched the wheel over, felt the rear
end start to slide, brought it out with a splash
of power and almost ran up the side of the cliff
as the car fishtailed. The brakes bit in, gouging
a furrow in the shoulder, then jumped to the pavement and held.

Somehow I had managed a sweeping curve
around the babe. For a few seconds she had been
living on stolen time because instead of getting
out of the way she had tried to stay in the beam
of the headlights. I sat there and let myself shake.
The butt that had fallen out of my mouth had
burned a hole in the leg of my pants and I flipped
it out the window. The stink of burned rubber
and brake lining hung in the air like smoke and
I was thinking of every damn thing I ever wanted
to say to a harebrained woman so I could have
it ready when I got my hands on her.

That was as far as I got. She was there in the
car beside me, the door slammed shut and she

said, "Thanks, mister."

Easy, feller, easy. She's a fruitcake. Don't plow her. Not yet. Hold your breath a minute, let it out easy, then maybe bend her over the fender and paddle her tail until she gets some sense in her head. Then boot her the hell out and make her walk the rest of the way home.

I fumbled out another cigarette, but she reached it before I did. For the first time I noticed her hands shaking as hard as mine were. I lit hers, got one out for me and lit that one too. "How stupid can you get?" I said.

She bit the words off. "Pretty stupid."

Behind me the lights of another car were reaching around a curve. Her eyes flicked back momentarily, fear pulling their corners tight. "You going to sit here all night, mister?"

"I don't know what I'm going to do. I'm thinking of throwing you over that cliff over there."

The headlights shone in the car through the rear window, bathed the roadway in light then swept on past. In the second that I had a good look at her she was rigid, her face frozen expressionlessly. When only the red dot of the taillight showed in front of us she let out her breath and leaned back against the seat.

In a way she was good-looking, but her face was more interesting than pretty. Wide-set eyes, large mouth, tawny hair that spilled onto her shoulders like melted butter. The rest of her was wrapped into a tailored trench coat that was belted around her waist and I remembered her standing

8

there in the road like something conjured up too quickly in a dream. A Viking. A damn-fool crazy Viking dame with holes in her head.

I kicked the stalled engine over, crawled through the gears and held on tight to the wheel until my brain started working right. An accident you don't mind. Those you halfway expect when you're holding seventy on a mountain road. But you don't expect a Viking dame to jump out of the dark at you while you're coming around a turn. I opened the window all the way down and drank in some of the air. "How'd you get up here?"

"What does it look like?"

"Like you got dumped." I looked at her quickly and saw her tongue snake out over her lips. "You picked the wrong guy to go out with."

"I'll know better the next time."

"Pull a trick like that last one and there won't be any next time. You damn near became a painting on the face of that rockslide."

"Thanks for the advice," she said sarcastically, "I'll be more careful."

"I don't give a hoot what you do as long as you don't get strained through my radiator."

She plucked the cigarette from her lips and blew a stream of smoke at the windshield. "Look, I'm grateful for the ride. I'm sorry I scared hell out of you. But if you don't mind just shut up and take me somewhere or let me out."

My mouth pulled back in a grin. A dame with nerve like that sure could've made a mess out of a guy before he gave her the boot. "Okay, girl,"

I said, "now it's my turn to be sorry. It's a hell of a place for anybody to be stranded and I guess I would have done the same thing. Almost. Where do you want to go?"

"Where're you going?"

"New York."

"All right, I'll go there."

"It's a big city, kid. Name the spot and I'll take you there."

Her eyes got cold. The frozen expression came back in her face. "Make it a subway station. The first one you come to will do."

Her tone wiped my grin away. I eased the car around another turn and settled down to a straightway, jamming hard on the gas. "Damn rape-happy dame. You think all guys are the same?"

"I . . ."

"Shut up."

I could feel her watching me. I knew when she dropped her eyes in her lap and knew when she looked back at me again. She started to say something and closed her mouth over the words. She turned to stare out of the window into the blackness of the night and one hand wiped her eyes. Let her bawl. Maybe she'd learn how to be a little polite.

Another car was coming up behind us. She saw it first and pressed back into the seat until it was past. It went on down the long incline ahead of us until its taillight merged and disappeared into the maze of neons that were part of the town below.

The tires whined on a turn and the force of it made her lean across the seat until our shoulders touched. She pulled away at the contact, braced herself until the car rocked back to level and edged into the corner. I looked at her, but she was staring out of the window, her face still cold.

I slowed to fifty coming into the town, then to thirty-five and held it. The sign along the road said HANAFIELD, POP. 3600, SPEED LIMIT 25. A quarter mile up the highway a flashing red light winked in our direction and I got on the brakes. There was a police car in the middle of the road and two uniformed cops stood alongside it checking the cars as they came by. The car that had passed us further back was just getting the okay to go on through and the flashlight was waving at me to make a full stop.

Trouble. Like the smoke over a cake of dry ice. You can't smell it but you can see it and watch it boil and seep around things and know that soon something's going to crack and shatter under the force of the horrible contraction. I looked at the dame and she was stiffly immobile, her lips held so tight her teeth showed, a scream held in her throat ready to let go.

I leaned out the car before I reached the cop and took the beam of his flash in the face before he lowered it. "Trouble, officer?"

His hat was pushed back on his head and a cigarette drooped from his mouth. The gun he wore hung cowboy style and for effect he draped his hand on its butt. "Where'd you come from, bud?"

11

A real cop, this guy. I wondered how much he paid for his appointment. "Coming down from Albany, officer. What's up?"

"See anybody along the road? Anybody hitchhiking?"

I felt her hand close over mine before I answered him. It closed and squeezed with a sudden warmth and urgency and in a quick movement she had taken my hand in hers and slid it under the trench coat and I felt the bare flesh of her thigh there, smooth and round, and when my fingers stiffened at the touch she thought I was hesitating and with a fluid motion moved her grip up my forearm and pulled my hand against her body where there was no doubting her meaning, then amplified it by squeezing her legs together gently to keep it there.

I said, "Not a thing, officer. My wife or me have been awake all the way and if anybody was there we sure would know about it. Maybe they came on ahead."

"Nobody came ahead, bud."

"Who were you looking for?"

"A dame. She escaped from some sanitarium upstate and hitched a ride down to a diner with a truck. When they started broadcasting a description she beat it outside and disappeared."

"Say, that's pretty serious. I wouldn't want to be the guy who picks her up. Is she dangerous?"

"All loonies are dangerous."

"What does she look like?"

"Tall blonde. That's about all we got on her. Nobody seems to remember what she was wearing."

12

"Oh. Well, okay for me to go?"

"Yeah, go on, beat it."

He walked back to the patrol car and I let out the clutch. I took my hand away slowly, keeping my eyes on the road. The town went by in a hurry, and on the other side I stepped on it again.

This time her hand crept up my arm and she slid across the seat until she was beside me. I said, "Get back where you came from sister. You didn't have to pull a stunt like that."

"I meant it."

"Thanks. It just wasn't necessary."

"You don't have to drop me at a subway station if you don't want to."

"I want to."

Her foot nudged mine off the gas pedal and the car lost headway. "Look," she said, and I turned my head. She had the coat wide open and was smiling at me. The coat, that's all, all the rest was sleekly naked. A Viking in satin skin. An invitation to explore the curves and valleys that lay nestled in the shadows and moved with her breathing. She squirmed in the seat and her legs made a beautifully obscene gesture and she smiled again.

She was familiar then. Not so much the person, but the smile. It was a forced, professional smile that looks warm as fire and really isn't anything at all. I reached over and flipped the coat closed. "You'll get cold," I said.

The smile twisted crookedly on her mouth. "Or is it that you're afraid because you think I'm not quite sane?"

13

"That doesn't bother me. Now shut up."

"No. Why didn't you tell him then?"

"Once when I was a kid I saw a dogcatcher about to net a dog. I kicked him in the shins, grabbed the pup and ran. The damn mutt bit me and got away, but I was still glad I did it."

"I see. But you believed what the man said."

"Anybody who jumps in front of a car isn't too bright. Now shut up."

The smile twisted a little more as if it weren't being forced. I looked at her, grinned at what had happened and shook my head. "I sure get some dillies," I said.

"What?"

"Nothing." I pulled the car off the road into the dull glare of the service-station sign and coasted up to the pumps. A guy came out of the building wiping his eyes and I told him to fill it up. I had to get out to unlock the gas cap and I heard the door open, then slam shut. The blonde went up to the building, walked inside and didn't come back until I was counting the money into the guy's hand.

When she got back in the car there was something there that hadn't been there before. Her face had softened and the frost had thawed until she seemed almost relaxed. Another car came by as we rolled off the gravel to the road only this time she didn't pay any attention to it at all. The coat was belted again, the flicker of a smile she gave me was real, and she put her head back against the seat and closed her eyes.

14

I didn't get it at all. All I knew was that when I hit the city I was going to pull up to the first subway station I saw, open the door, say good-by, then check on the papers until I found where somebody had put her back on the shelf again. I thought that. I wished I could mean it. All I felt was the trouble like the smoke over dry ice and it was seeping all over me.

For five minutes she sat and watched the edge of the road, then said, "Cigarette?" I shook one into her hand and shoved the dashboard lighter in. When it was lit she dragged in deeply and watched the gray haze swirl off the windows. "Are you wondering what it's all about?" she asked me.

"Not particularly."

"I was . . ." she hesitated, "in a sanitarium." The second pull on the butt nearly dragged the lit end down to her fingers. "They forced me to go there. They took away my clothes to make me stay there."

I nodded as if I understood.

She shook her head slowly, getting the meaning of my gesture. "Maybe I'll find somebody who will understand. I thought maybe . . . you would."

I went to say something. It never came out. The moon that had been hidden behind the clouds came out long enough to bathe the earth in a quick shower of pale yellow light that threw startlingly long shadows across the road and among those dark fingers was one that seemed darker still and moved with a series of jerks and a roar of sound that evolved into a dark sedan cutting in front of us.

15

For the second time I heard the scream of tires on pavement and with it another scream not from the tires as metal tore into metal with a nasty tearing sound as splintering glass made little incongruous musical high lights above it all.

I kicked the door open and came out of the car in time to see the men piling out of the sedan. The trouble was all around us and you couldn't walk away from it. But I didn't expect it to be as bad as that. The gun in the guy's hand spit out a tongue of flame that lanced into the night and the bullet's banshee scream matched the one that was still going on behind me.

He never got another shot out because my fist split his face open. I went into the one behind him as something hissed through the air behind my head then hissed again and thudded against my shoulders. My arm went on that one and I spun around to get him with my foot. It was just a little too late. There was another hiss of something whipping through the air and whatever it was, it caught me across the forehead and for a second before all time and distance went I thought I was going to be sick and the hate for those bastards oozed out of my skin like sweat.

I didn't lie there for long. The pain that pounded across my head was too sharp, too damn deep. It was a hard, biting pain that burst in my ears with every heartbeat, sending a blinding white light flashing into my eyes even though they were squeezed shut.

In back of it all was the muffled screaming, the

choked-off sobs, the cadence of harsh, angry voices biting out words that were indistinguishable at first. The motor of a car chewed into the sounds and there was more jangling of metal against metal. I tried to get up, but it was only my mind that could move. The rest of me was limp and dead. When the sense of movement did happen it wasn't by command but because arms had me around the waist and my feet and hands scraped cold concrete. Somewhere during those seconds the screaming had been chopped off, the voices had ceased and a certain pattern of action had begun to form.

You don't think at a time like that. You try to remember first, to collect events that led up to the end, to get things relatively assorted in their proper places so you can look at and study them with a bewildered sort of wonder that is saturated with pain, to find a beginning and an end. But nothing makes sense, all you feel is a madness and hate that rises and grows into a terrible frenzy that even wipes out the pain and you want to kill something so bad your brain is on fire. Then you realize that you can't even do that and the fire explodes into consciousness because of it and you can see once more.

They had left me on the floor. There were my feet and my hands, immobile lumps jutting in front of my body. The backs of the hands and the sleeves were red and sticky. The taste of the stickiness was in my mouth too. Something moved and a pair of shoes shuffled into sight so I knew I wasn't alone. The floor in front of my feet stretched out into other shoes and the lower halves of legs. Shiny shoes marred with a film of dust. One with a jagged scratch across the toe. Four separate pairs of feet all pointing toward the same direction and when my eyes followed them I saw her in the chair and saw what they were doing to her.

She had no coat on now and her skin had an unholy whiteness about it, splotched with deeper colors. She was sprawled in the chair, her mouth making uncontrollable mewing sounds. The hand with the pliers did something horrible to her and the mouth opened without screaming.

A voice said, "Enough. That's enough."

"She can still talk," the other one answered.

"No, she's past it. I've seen it happen before. We were silly to go this far, but we had no choice."

"Listen . . ."

"I'll give the orders. You listen."

The feet moved back a little. "All right, go ahead. But so far we don't know any more than we did before."

"That's satisfactory. What we do know is still more than anyone else. There are other ways and at least she won't be talking to the wrong ones. She'll have to go now. Everything is ready?"

"Yeah." It was a disgusted acknowledgment. "The guy too?"

"Naturally. Take them out to the road."

"It's a shame to dress her."

"You pig. Do what you're told. You two, help carry them out. We've spent enough time on this operation."

I could feel my mouth working to get some words out. Every filthy name I could think of for them was stuck in my throat. I couldn't even raise my eyes above their knees to see their faces and all I could do was hear them, hear everything they said and keep the sound of their voices spilling over in my ears so that when I heard them again I wouldn't need to look at their faces to know I was killing the right ones. The bastards, the dirty lousy bastards!

Hands went under my knees and shoulders and for a second I thought I would see what I wanted to see, but the hate inside me sent the blood beating to my head bringing back the pain and it was like a black curtain being pulled closed across my mind. Once it drew back hesitatingly and I saw my car on the side of the road, the rear end lifted with a jack and red flares set in front and in back of it.

Clever, I thought. Very clever of them. If anybody passed they'd see a car in trouble with warning signals properly placed and the driver obviously gone into town for help. Nobody would stop to investigate. Then the thought passed into the darkness as quickly as it came.

It was like a sleep that you awaken from because you had been sleeping cramped up. It was a forced awakening that hurts and you hear yourself groan as you try to straighten out. *Then suddenly there's an immediate sharpness to the awakening as you realize that it hadn't been a bad dream after all, but something alive and terrifying instead.*

19

She was there beside me in the car, the open coat framing her nakedness. Her head lolled against the window, the eyes staring sightlessly at the ceiling. She jerked and fell against me.

But not because she was alive! The car was moving ahead as something rammed into the rear of it!

Somehow I got myself up, looked over the wheel into the splash of light ahead of me and saw the edge of the cliff short feet away and even as I reached for the door the wheels went over the edge through the ready-made gap in the retaining wall and the nose dipped down into an incredible void.

Chapter Two

"Mike . . ."

I turned my head toward the sound. The motion brought a wave of silent thunder with it like the surf crashing on a beach. I heard my name again, a little clearer this time.

"Mike . . ."

My eyes opened. The light hurt, but I kept them open. For a minute she was just a dark blur, then the fuzzy edges went away and the blue became beautiful. "Hello, kitten," I said.

Velda's mouth parted in a slow smile that had all the happiness in the world wrapped up in it. "Glad to see you back, Mike."

"It's . . . good to be back. I'm surprised . . . I got here."

"So are a lot of people."

"I . . ."

"Don't talk. The doctor said to keep you quiet if you woke up. Otherwise he'd chase me away."

I tried to grin at her and she dropped her hand over mine. It was warm and soft with a gentle pressure that said everything was okay. I held it for a long time and if she took it away I never knew about it because when I awoke again it was still there.

The doctor was an efficient little man who poked and prodded with stiff fingers while he watched the expression on my face. He seemed to reel off yards of tape and gauze to dress me in and went away looking satisfied as though he had made me to start with.

Before he closed the door he turned around, glanced at his watch and said, "Thirty minutes, miss. I want him to sleep again."

Velda nodded and squeezed my hand. "Feel better?"

"Somewhat."

"Pat's outside. Shall I ask him to come in?"

". . . Yeah."

She got up and went to the door. I heard her speak to somebody, then there he was grinning at me foolishly, shaking his head while he looked me over.

"Like my outfit?" I said.

"Great. On you white looks good. Three days ago I was figuring I'd have to finance a new tux to bury the corpse in."

Nice guy, Pat. A swell cop, but he was getting one hell of a sense of humor. When his words sunk in I felt my forehead wrinkling under the turban. "Three days?"

He nodded and draped himself in the big chair beside the bed. "You got it Monday. This is Thursday."

"Brother!"

"I know what you mean."

He glanced at Velda. A quick look that had something behind it I didn't get. She bit her lip, her teeth glistening against the magenta ripeness of her mouth, then nodded in assent.

Pat said, "Can you remember what happened, Mike?"

I knew the tone. He tried to cover it but he didn't make out. It was the soft trouble tone, falsely light yet direct and insistent. He knew I had caught it and his eyes dropped while he fiddled with his coat. "I remember."

"Care to tell me about it?"

"Why?"

This time he tried to look surprised. That didn't work either. "No reason."

"I had an accident, that's all."

"That's all?"

I got the grin out again and turned it on Velda. She was worried, but not too worried to smile back. "Maybe you can tell me what's cooking, kid. He won't."

"I'll let Pat tell you. He's been pretty obscure with me too."

"It's your ball, Pat," I said.

He stared at me a minute, then: "Right now I wish you weren't so sick. I'm the cop and you're the one who's supposed to answer questions."

"Sure, but I'm standing on my constitutional rights. It's very legal. Go ahead."

"All right, just keep your voice down or that medic will be hustling me out of here. If we weren't

23

buddies I couldn't get within a mile of you with that watchdog around."

"What's the pitch?"

"You're not to be questioned . . . yet."

"Who wants to question me?"

"Among other law enforcement agencies, some government men. That accident of yours occurred in New York State, but right now you happen to be just over the state line in a Jersey hospital. The New York State Troopers will be looking forward to seeing you, plus some county cops from upstate a ways."

"I think I'll stay in Jersey a while."

"Those government men don't care what state you're in."

And there was that tone again.

"Suppose you explain," I said.

I watched the play of expression across his face to see what he was trying to hide. He looked down at his fingers and pared his nails absently. "You were lucky to get out of the car alive. The door sprung when it hit the side of the drop and you were thrown clear. They found you wrapped around some bushes. If the car hadn't sprayed the place with burning gas you might still be there. Fortunately, it attracted some motorists who went down to see what happened. Not much was left of the car at all."

"There was a dame in there," I told him.

"I'm coming to that." His head came up and his eyes searched my face. "She was dead. She's been identified."

"As an escapee from a sanitarium," I finished.

It didn't catch him a bit off base. "Those county cops were pretty sore about it when they found out. Why did you pass them up?"

"I didn't like their attitude."

He nodded as if that explained it. Hell, it did.

"You better start thinking before you pull stunts like that, Mike."

"Why?"

"The woman didn't die in the crash."

"I figured as much."

Maybe I shouldn't have been so calm about it. His lips got tight all of a sudden and the fingernails he had been tending disappeared into balled-up fists. "Damn it, Mike, what are you into? Do you realize what kind of a mess you've been fooling around with?"

"No. I'm waiting for you to tell me."

"That woman was under surveillance by the feds. She was part of something big that I don't know about myself and she was committed to the institution to recover so she could do some tall talking to a closed session of Congress. There was a police guard outside her door and on the grounds of the place. Right now the Washington boys are hopping and it looks like the finger is pointed at you. As far as they're concerned you got her out of there and knocked her off."

I lay there and looked at the ceiling. A crack in the plaster zigzagged across the room and disappeared under the molding. "What do *you* think, Pat?"

"I'm waiting to hear you say it."

"I already said it."

"An accident?" His smile was too damn sarcastic. "It was an accident to have a practically naked woman in your car? It was an accident to lie your way through a police roadblock? It was an accident to have her dead before your car went through the wall? You'll have to do better than that, pal. I know you too well. If accidents happen they go the way you want them to."

"It was an accident."

"Mike, look . . . you can call it what you like. I'm a cop and I'm in a position to help you out if there's trouble, but if you don't square away with me I'm not going to do a thing. When those Federal boys move in you're going to have to do better than that accident story."

Velda moved her hand up to my chin and turned my head so she could look at me. "It's big, Mike," she said. "Can you fill in the details?" She was so completely serious it was almost funny. I felt like kissing the tip of her nose and sending her out to play, but her eyes were pleading with me.

I said, "It was an accident. I picked her up on the way down from Albany. I don't know a thing about her, but she seemed like a nervy kid in a jam and I didn't like the snotty way that cop acted when he stopped the car. So I went on through. We got down maybe ten miles when a sedan pulled out from the side of the road and nudged me to a stop. Now here's the part you won't believe. I got out sore as hell and somebody took a shot at me. It missed, but I got sapped and sapped so beautifully I never came completely out of it. I don't know where the hell they took us, but wherever it was they tried to force something out of the dame. She never came across. Those lads were anxious to get rid of her and me too so they piled us in the car and gave it a shove over the cliff."

"Who are they?" Pat asked.

"Damned if I know. Five or six guys."

"Can you identify them?"

"Not by their faces. Maybe if I heard them speak."

I didn't mean maybe at all. I could still hear every syllable they spoke and those voices would talk in my mind until I died. Or they did.

The silence was pretty deep. The puzzle was on Velda's face. "Is that all?" she asked me.

Pat spoke out of the stillness, his voice soft again. "That's all he's going to tell anybody." He got up and stood by the bed. "If that's the way you want it, I'll play along. I hope like hell you're telling me the truth."

"But you're afraid I'm not, is that it?"

"Uh-huh. I'll check on it. I can still see some holes in it."

"For instance?"

"The gap in the guard rail. No slow-moving car did that. It was a fresh break, too."

"Then they did it with their car purposely."

"Maybe. Where was your heap while they were working the woman over?"

"Nicely parked off the road with a jack under

27

it and flares set out."

"Clever thought."

"I thought so too," I said.

"Who could ever find anybody who noticed the flares? They'd just breeze right on by."

"That's right."

Pat hesitated, glanced at Velda, then back to me again. "You're going to stick with that story?"

"What else?"

"Okay, I'll check on it. I hope you aren't making any mistakes. Good night now. Take it easy." He started to the door.

I said, "I'll do my own checking when I'm up, Pat."

He stopped with his hand on the knob. "Don't keep asking for trouble, kid. You have enough right now."

"I don't like to get sapped and tossed over a cliff."

"Mike . . ."

"See you around, Pat." He shot me a wry grin and left. I picked up Velda's hand and looked at her watch. "You have five minutes left out of the thirty. How do you want to spend it?"

The seriousness washed away all at once. She was a big, luscious woman smiling at me with a mouth that was only inches away and coming closer each second. Velda. Tall, with hair like midnight. Beautiful, so it hurt to look at her.

Her hands were soft on my face and her mouth a hot, hungry thing that tried to drink me down. Even through the covers I could feel the firm pressure of her breasts, live things that caressed me of their own accord. She took her mouth away reluctantly so I could kiss her neck and run my lips across her shoulders.

"I love you, Mike," she said. "I love everything about you even when you're all fouled up with trouble." She traced a path down my cheek with her finger. "Now what do you want me to do?"

"Get your nose to the ground, kitten," I told her. "Find out what the hell this is all about. Take a check on that sanitarium and get a line into Washington if you can."

"That won't be easy."

"They can't keep secrets in the Capitol, baby. There will be rumors."

"And what will you do?"

"Try to make those feds believe that accident yarn."

Her eyes widened a little. "You mean . . . it didn't happen that way?"

"Uh-uh. I mean it did. It's just that nobody's going to believe it."

I patted her hand and she straightened up from the bed. I watched her walk toward the door, taking in every feline motion of her body. There was something lithe and animal-like in the way she swung her hips, a jungle tautness to her shoulders. Cleopatra might have had it. Josephine might have had it. But they never had it like she had it.

I said, "Velda . . ." and she turned around, knowing damn well what I was going to say. "Show me your legs."

She grinned impishly, her eyes dancing, standing in a pose no calendar artist could duplicate. She was a Circe, a lusty temptress, a piece of living statuary on display, that only one guy would be able to see. The hem of the dress came up quickly, letting the roundness under the nylon evolve into a magical symmetry, then the nylon ended in the quick whiteness of her thigh and I said, "Enough, kitten. Quit it."

Before I could say anything else she laughed down deep, threw me a kiss and grinned, "Now you know how Ulysses felt."

Now I knew. The guy was a sucker. He should have jumped ship.

Chapter Three

It was Monday again, a rainy, dreary Monday that was a huge wet muffler draped over the land. I watched it through the window and felt the taste of it in my mouth. The door opened and the doctor said, "Ready?"

I turned away from the window and squashed out the cigarette. "Yeah. Are they waiting for me downstairs?"

His tongue showed pink through his lips for a moment and he nodded. "I'm afraid so."

I picked my hat up from the chair and walked across the room. "Thanks for keeping them off my back so long, doc."

"It was a necessary thing. You had quite a blow, young man. There still may be complications." He held the door open for me, waved toward the elevator down the hall and waited silently beside me for it to crawl up to the floor. He took his place beside me on the way down, once letting his eyes edge over so he could watch me.

We got out in the lobby, shook hands briefly and I went to the cashier's window. She checked my name, told me everything had been paid for by my secretary, then handed me a receipted bill.

When I turned around they were all standing there politely, hats in their hands. Young guys with old eyes. Sharp. Junior executive types. Maybe you could pick them out of a crowd but most likely you couldn't. No gun bulges under the suit jackets, no high-top shoes with arch supports. Not too fat, not too lean. Faces you wouldn't want to lie past. Junior executives all right, but in J. Edgar Hoover's organization.

The tall guy in the blue pin stripe said, "Our car is out front, Mr. Hammer." I fell in beside him with the others bringing up on the flank and went out to get driven home. We took the Lincoln Tunnel across into New York, cut east on Forty-first then took Ninth Avenue downtown to the modern gray building they used for operational headquarters.

They were real nice, those boys. They took my hat and coat, shoved up a chair for me to sit in, asked if I felt well enough to talk and when I told them sure, suggested that maybe I'd like a lawyer present.

I grinned at that one. "Nope, just ask questions and I'll do what I can to answer them. But thanks anyway."

The tall one nodded and looked over my head at someone else. "Bring in the file," he said. In back of me a door opened and closed. He leaned forward on the desk, his fingers laced together. "Now, Mr. Hammer, we'll get down to cases. You're completely aware of the situation?"

"I'm aware that no situation exists," I said bluntly.

"Really?"

I said, "Look, friend. You may be the F.B.I. and I may be up to my ears in something you're interested in, but let's get something straight. I don't get bluffed. Not even by the feds. I came here of my own free will. I'm fairly well acquainted with the law. The reason I didn't squawk about coming down here was because I wanted to get straightened out all the way around and quick because I have things to do when I leave and I don't want any cops tagging me around. That much understood?"

He didn't answer me right away. The door opened and closed again and a hand passed a folder over my shoulder. He took it, flipped it open and glanced through it. But he wasn't reading it. He knew the damn thing by heart. "It says here you're pretty tough, Mr. Hammer."

"Some people seem to think so."

"Several close brushes with the law, I notice."

"Notice the result."

"I have. I imagine your license can be waivered if we want to press the issue."

I dragged out my deck of Luckies and flipped one loose. "I said I'd cooperate. You can quit trying to bluff me."

His eyes came over the edge of the folder. "We're not bluffing. The police in upstate New York want you. Would you sooner talk to them?"

It was getting a little tiresome. "If you want.

33

They can't do anything more than talk either."

"You ran a roadblock."

"Wrong, chum, I stopped for it."

"But you did lie to the officer who questioned you?"

"Certainly. Hell, I wasn't under oath. If he had any sense he would have looked at the dame and questioned her." I let the smoke drift out of my mouth toward the ceiling.

"The dead woman in your car . . ."

"You're getting lame," I said. "You know damn well I didn't kill her."

His smile was a lazy thing. "How do we know?"

"Because I didn't. I don't know how she died, but if she was shot you've already checked my apartment and found my gun there. You've already taken a paraffin test on me and it came out negative. If she was choked the marks on her neck didn't match the spread of my hands. If she was stabbed . . ."

"Her skull was crushed by a blunt instrument," he put in quietly.

And I said just as quietly, "It matched the indentation in my own skull then and you know it."

If I thought he was going to get sore I was wrong. He twisted his smile in a little deeper and leaned back in the chair with his head cradled in his hands. Behind me someone coughed to cover up a laugh.

"Okay, Mr. Hammer, you seem to know everything. Sometimes we can break even the tough ones down without much trouble. We did all the

34

things you mentioned before you regained consciousness. Were you guessing?"

I shook my head. "Hell, no. I don't underestimate cops. I've made a pretty good living in the racket myself. Now if there's anything you'd really like to know I'd be glad to give it to you."

His mouth pursed in thought a minute. "Captain Chambers gave us a complete report on things. The details checked . . . and your part in it seems to fit your nature. Please understand something, Mr. Hammer. We're not after you. If your part was innocent enough that's as far as we need to go. It's just that we can't afford to pass up any angles."

"Good. Then I'm clear?"

"As far as we're concerned."

"I suppose they have a warrant out for me upstate."

"We'll take care of it."

"Thanks."

"There's just one thing . . ."

"Yeah?"

"From your record you seem to be a pretty astute sort of person. What's your opinion on this thing?"

"Since when do you guys deal in guesswork?"

"When that's all we have to go on."

I dropped the cigarette into the ash tray on the desk and looked at him. "The dame knew something she shouldn't have. Whoever pulled it were smart cookies. I think the sedan that waited for us was one that passed us up right after I took her aboard. It was a bad spot to try anything so they went ahead and picked the right one. She wouldn't talk so they bumped her. I imagine it was supposed to look like an accident."

"That's right, it was."

"Now do you mind if I ask one?"

"No. Go right ahead."

"Who was she?"

"Berga Torn." My eyes told him to finish it and he shrugged his shoulder. "She was a taxi dancer, night-club entertainer, friend of boys on the loose and anything else you can mention where sex is concerned."

A frown pulled at my forehead. "I don't get it."

"You're not supposed to, Mr. Hammer." A freeze clouded up his eyes. It told me that was as much as he was about to say and I was all through. I could go now and thanks. Thanks a lot.

I got up and pulled my hat on. One of the boys held the door open for me. I turned around and grinned at him. "I will, feller," I said.

"What?"

"Get it." My grin got bigger. "Then somebody else is going to get it."

I pulled the door closed and got out in the hall. I stood there a minute leaning up against the wall until the pounding in my forehead stopped and the lights left my eyes. There was a dry sour taste in my mouth that made me want to spit, a nasty hate buzzing around my head that pulled my lips tight across my teeth and brought the voices back in my ears and then I felt better because I knew that I'd never forget them and that some day I'd hear them again only this time they'd choke out the last sound they'd ever make.

I took the elevator downstairs, called a cab and gave him Pat's office address. The cop on the desk told me to go ahead up and when I walked in Pat was sitting there waiting for me trying on a friendly smile for size.

He said, "How did it go, Mike?"

"It was a rotten pitch." I hooked a chair over with my foot and sat down. "I don't know what the act was for, but they sure wasted time."

"They *never* waste time."

"Then why the ride?"

"Checking. I gave them the facts they hadn't already picked up."

"They didn't seem to do anything about it."

"I didn't expect them to." He dropped the chair forward on all four legs. "I suppose you asked them some things too."

"Yeah, I know the kid's name. Berga Torn."

"That all?"

"Part of her history. What's the rest?"

Pat dropped his eyes and stared at his hands. When he was ready to speak he looked up at me, his face a study in caution. "Mike . . . I'm going to give you some information. The reason I'm doing it is because you're likely to fish around and find it yourself if I don't and interference is one thing we can't have."

"Go ahead."

"You've heard of Carl Evello?"

I nodded.

"Evello is the boy behind the powers. The last senatorial investigations turned up a lot of big names in the criminal world, but they never turned up his. That's how big he is. The others are pretty big too, but not like him."

I felt my eyebrows go up. "I didn't know he was that big. Where does it come from?"

"Nobody seems to know. A lot is suspected, but until there's plenty of concrete evidence, no charges are going to be passed around even by me. Just take my word for it that the guy is big. Now . . . they want him. They want him bad and when they get him all the other big boys are going to fall too."

"So what."

"Berga Torn was his mistress for a while."

It started to make sense now. I said, "So she had something on the guy?"

Pat shrugged disgustedly. "Who knows? She was supposed to have had something. She can't talk. When they were giving her the business as you said they were trying to get it out of her."

"You figure they were Carl's men then."

"Evidently."

"What about the sanitarium she was in?"

"She was there under the advice of her doctor," Pat said. "She was going to testify to the committee and under the strain almost had a nervous breakdown. All the committee hearings were tied up until she was released."

I said, "That's a pretty picture, kid. Where do I come in?"

Little light lines seemed to grow around his eyes. "You don't. You stay out of it."

"Nuts."

"Okay, hero, then let's break it down. There's no reason for you to mess around. It was just an accident that got you into it anyway. There's nothing much you can do and anything you *try* to do is damn well going to be resented by all the agencies concerned."

I gave him my best big grin. All the teeth. Even the eyes. "You flatter me."

"Don't get smart, Mike."

"I'm not."

"All right, you're a bright boy and I know how you work. I'm just trying to stop any trouble before it starts."

"Pal, you got it wrong," I said, "it's already started, remember? I got patted between the eyes, a dame got bumped and my car is wrecked." I stood up and looked down at him feeling things changing in my smile. "Maybe I have too much pride, but I don't let anybody get away with that kind of stuff. I'm going to knock the crap out of somebody for all that and if it gets up to Evello it's okay with me."

Pat's hand came down on the edge of the desk. "Damn it, Mike, why don't you get a little sense in your head? You . . ."

"Look . . . suppose somebody took you for a patsy. What would you do?"

39

"That didn't happen."

"No . . . but it happened to me. Those boys aren't that tough that they can get away with it. Damn it, Pat, you ought to know me better than that."

"I do, that's why I'm asking you to lay off. What do I have to do, appeal to your patriotism?"

"Patriotism, my back. I don't give a damn if Congress, the President and the Supreme Court told me to lay off. They're only men and they didn't get sapped and dumped over a cliff. You don't play games with guys who pull that kind of stuff. The feds can be as cagey as they like, but when they wrap the bunch up what happens? So they testify. Great. Costello testified and I can show you where he committed perjury in the minutes of the hearing. What happened? Yeah . . . you know what happened as well as I do. They're too big to do anything with. They got too much dough and too much power and if they talk too many people are going to go under. Well, the hell with 'em. There are a bunch of guys who drove a sedan I want to see again. I don't know what they look like, but I'll know them when I see them. If the feds beat me to 'em it's okay by me, but I'll wait, pal. If I don't reach them first I'll wait until they get through testifying or serving that short sentence those babies seem to draw and when I do you won't be having much trouble from them again ever."

"You have it all figured?"

"Uh-huh. Right down to the self-defense plea."

"You won't get far."

I grinned at him again. "You know better than that, don't you?"

For a moment the seriousness left his face. His mouth cracked in a grin. "Yeah," he said, "that's what I'm afraid of."

"That wasn't any ordinary kill."

"No."

"They were a bunch of cold-blooded bastards. You should have seen what they did to that kid before they killed her."

"Nothing showed on her body . . . or what was left of it after the fire."

"It was there. It wasn't very pretty." I stared at him hard. "It changes something in the way you were thinking."

His eyes came up speculatively.

"They didn't give her the works to see how much she knew. They were after something she knew and they didn't. She was the key to something."

Pat's face was grave. "And you're going after it?"

"What did you expect?"

"I don't know, Mike." He wiped his hand across his eyes. "I guess I didn't expect you to take it lying down." He turned his head and glanced out of the window at the rain. "But since it's going to be that way you might as well know this much. Those government boys are shrewd apples. They know your record and how you work. They even know how you think. Don't expect any help from this end. If you cross those boys you're going to wind up in the can."

"You have your orders?" I asked him.

"In writing. From pretty high authority." His eyes met mine. "I was told to pass the news on to you if you acted up."

I stood up and fiddled with my pack of butts. "Great guys. They want to do it all alone. They're too smart to need help."

"They have the equipment and manpower," Pat said defensively.

"Yeah, sure, but they don't have the attitude." A grimace pulled at my mouth. "They want to make a public example out of those big boys. They want to see them sweat it out behind bars. Nuts to that. Those lads in the sedan don't give a hoot for authority. They don't give a damn for you, me or anybody besides themselves. They only respect one thing."

"Say it."

"A gun in their bellies that's going off and splashing their guts around the room. That kind of attitude they respect." I stuck my hat on my head, keeping it back off the blue lump between my eyes. "See you around, Pat," I said.

"Maybe, maybe not," he said to my back.

I went downstairs into the rain and waited there until a cab came along.

Unless you knew they were there you'd never notice it. Just little things out of place here and there. A streak through the dust where a coat sleeve dragged, an ash tray not quite in place, the rubber seal around the refrigerator door hanging because they didn't know it was loose and had to be stuffed back by hand.

The .45 was still hanging in the closet, but this time there was a thumbprint on the side where I knew I had wiped it before I stuck it away. I picked the rig off the hook and laid it on the table. The Washington boys were pretty good at that sort of thing. I started to whistle a tuneless song as I climbed out of my jacket when I noticed the wastebasket beside the dresser. There was a cigarette butt in the bottom with the brand showing and it wasn't my brand. I picked it up, stared at it, threw it back and went on whistling. I stopped when the thought of it jelled, picked up the phone and dialed the super's number downstairs.

I said, "This is Mike Hammer, John. Did you let some men in up here?"

He hedged with, "Men? You know, Mr. Hammer, I . . ."

"It's okay, I had a talk with them. I just wanted to check on it."

"Well, in that case . . . they had a warrant. You know what they were? They were F.B.I. men."

"Yeah, I know."

"They said I shouldn't mention it."

"You're sure about it?"

"Sure as anything. They had a city cop along too."

"What about anybody else?"

43

"Nobody else, Mr. Hammer. I wouldn't let a soul in up there, you know that."

"Okay, John. Thanks." I hung up the phone and looked around again.

Somebody else had gone through the apartment. They had done a good job too. But not quite as good as the feds. They had left their trademark around.

The smoke that was trouble started to boil up around me again. You couldn't see it and you couldn't smell it, but it was there. I started whistling again and picked up the .45.

Chapter Four

She came in at half-past eleven. She used the key I had given her a long time ago and walked into the living room bringing with her the warmth and love for life that was like turning on the light.

I said, "Hello, beautiful," and I didn't have to say anything more because there was more in the words than the sound of my voice and she knew it.

She started to smile slowly and her mouth made a kiss. Our lips didn't have to touch. She flung that warmth across the room and I caught it. Velda said, "Ugly face. You're uglier now than you were but I love you more than ever."

"So I'm ugly. Underneath I'm beautiful."

"Who can dig down that deep?" she grinned. Then added, "Except me, maybe."

"*Just* you, honey," I said.

The smile that played around her mouth softened a moment, then she slipped out of the coat and threw it across the back of a chair.

I could never get tired of looking at her, I thought. She was everything you needed just when you needed it, a bundle of woman whose emotions could be hard or soft or terrifying, but whatever they were it was what you wanted. She was the lush beauty of the jungle, the sleek sophisticate of the city. Like I said, to me she was everything, and the dull light of the room was reflected in the ring on her finger that I had given her.

I watched her go to the kitchen and open a pair of beer cans. I watched while she sat down, took the frosted can from her and watched while she sipped the top off hers and felt a sudden stirring when her tongue flicked the foam from her lips.

Then she said what I knew she was going to say. "This one's too big, Mike."

"It is?"

Her eyes drew a line across the floor and up my body until they were staring hard into mine. "I was busy while you were in the hospital, Mike. I didn't just let things wait until you got well. This isn't murder as you've known it before. It was planned, organizational killing and it's so big that even the city authorities are afraid of it. The thing has ballooned up to a point where it's Federal and even then it's touching such high places that the feds have to move carefully."

"So?" I let it hang there and pulled on the can of beer.

"It doesn't make any difference what I think?"

I set the can on the end table and made the three-ring pattern on the label. "What you think makes a lot of difference, kitten, but when it comes to making the decisions I'll make them on what I think. I'm a man. So I'm just one man, but as

46

long as I have a brain of my own to use and experience and knowledge to draw on to form a decision I'll keep on making them myself."

"And you're going after them?"

"Would you like me better if I didn't?"

The grin crept back through the seriousness on her face. "No." Then her eyes laughed at me too. "Ten million dollars' worth of men and equipment bucking another multi-million outfit and you elect yourself to step in and clean up. But then, you're a man." She sipped from the beer can again, then said, "But what a man. I'll be glad when you step off that bachelorhood pedestal and move over to where I have a little control over you."

"Think you ever will?"

"No, but at least I'll have something to bargain with," she laughed. "I'd like to have you around for a long time without worrying about you."

"I feel the same way myself, Velda. It's just that some things come first."

"I know, but let me warn you. From now on you're going to be up against a scheming woman."

"That's been tried before."

"Not like this."

"Yeah," I said, and finished the beer. I waited until she put hers down too, then shook out a Lucky and tossed the pack over to her. "What did you pick up?"

"A few details. I found a trucker who passed your car where they had it parked with the flares fore and aft. The guy stopped, and when he saw nobody around he went on. The nearest phone was three miles down the road in a diner and he was surprised when nobody had shown up there because he hadn't seen anyone walking. The girl in the diner knew about an abandoned shack a few hundred yards from the spot and I went there. The place was alive with feds."

"Great."

"That's hardly the word for it." She squirmed in the chair and ran her fingers through her hair, the deep ebony of it rubbed to a soft glow in the pale lamplight. "They held me for a while, questioned me, and released me with a warning that had teeth in it."

"They find anything?"

"From what I could see, nothing. They backtracked the same way that I did and anything they found just supported what you had already told them.

"There's a catch in it though," she said. "The shack was a good fifty yards in from the highway and covered with brush. You could light the place up and it wouldn't be seen, and unless you knew where to look you'd never find it."

"It was too convenient to be coincidental, you mean?"

"Much too convenient."

I spit out a stream of smoke and watched it flow around the empty beer can. "That doesn't make sense. The kid was running away. How'd they know which direction she'd pick out?"

"They wouldn't, but how would they know where that shack was?"

48

"Who'd the shack belong to?"

A frown creased her forehead and she shook her head. "That's another catch. The place is on state property. It's been there for twenty years. One thing I did learn while I was being questioned was that aside from its recent use the place had no signs of occupancy at all. There were dates carved in the doorpost and the last one was 1937."

"Anything else?"

Velda shook her head slowly. "I saw your car. Or what's left of it."

"Poor old baby. The last of the original hot rods."

"Mike . . ."

I finished the beer and put the empty down on the table. "Yeah?"

"What are you going to do?"

"Guess."

"Tell me."

I had a long pull on the smoke and dropped the butt into the can. "They killed a dame and tried to frame me for it. They wrecked my heap and put me in the hospital. They're figuring us all for suckers and don't give a hang who gets hurt. The slobs, the miserable slobs." I rammed my fist against my palm until it stung. "I'm going to find out what the score is, kid. Then a lot of heads are going to roll."

"One of them might be yours, Mike."

"Yeah, one of 'em might, but it sure won't be the first to go. And you know something? They're worried, whoever they are. They read the papers and things didn't quite happen like they wanted them to. The law of averages bucked 'em for a change and instead of getting a sucker to frame they got me. Me. That they didn't like because I'm not just the average joe and they're smart enough to figure out an angle."

Her face pulled tight and the question was in her eyes. "They were up here looking around," I said.

"Mike!"

"Oh, I don't know what they were after, but I don't think they knew either. But you can bet on this, they went through this place because they thought I had something they wanted and just because they didn't find it doesn't mean they think I haven't got it. They'll be back. The next time I won't be in an emergency ward."

"But what could it be?"

"Beats me, but they tried to kill two people to find out. Whether I like it or not I'm in this thing as deep as that dame was." I grinned at Velda sitting there. "And I like it, too. I hate the guts of those people. I hate them so bad it's coming out of my skin. I'm going to find out who 'they' are and why and then they've had it."

A note of sarcasm crept into her voice. "Just like always, isn't that right?"

"No," I said, "Maybe not. Maybe this time I'll do it differently. Just for the fun of it."

Velda's hands were drawn tight on the arms of the chair. "I don't like you this way, Mike."

"Neither do a lot of people. They know something just like their own names. They know I'm not going to sit on my fanny and wait for something to happen. They know from now on they're going to have to be so careful they won't even be able to spit because I'm going to get closer and closer until I have them on the dirty end of a stick. They know it and I know it too."

"It makes you a target."

"Kitten, it sure does and that I go for. If that's one way of pulling 'em inside shooting range I'm plenty glad to be a target."

Her face relaxed and she sat back. For a long minute neither one of us spoke. She sat there with her head against the cushion staring at the ceiling, then, "Mike, I have news for you."

The way she said it made me look up. "Give."

"Any shooting that's to be done won't be done by you."

A muscle in my face twitched.

Velda reached in her jacket pocket and came out with an envelope. She flipped it across the room and I caught it. "Pat brought it in this morning. He couldn't do a thing about it, so don't get teed off at him."

I pulled the flap out and fingered the sheet loose. It was very brief and to the point. No quibbling. No doubting the source. The letterhead was all very official and I was willing to bet that for the one sheet they sent me a hundred more made up the details of why the thing should be sent.

It was a very simple order telling me I no longer had a license to carry a gun and temporarily my

51

state-granted right to conduct private investigations was suspended. There was no mention of a full or partial refund of my two-hundred-buck fee for said license to said state.

So I laughed. I folded the sheet back into the envelope and laid it on the table. "They want me to do it the hard way," I said.

"They don't want you to do it at all. From now on you're a private citizen and nothing else and if they catch you with a gun you get it under the Sullivan law."

"This happened once before, remember?"

Velda nodded slowly. There was no expression at all on her face. "That's right, but they forgot about me. Then I had a P.I. ticket and a license for a gun too. This time they didn't forget."

"Smart boys."

"Very." She closed her eyes again and let her head drop back. "We're going to have it rough."

"Not we, girl. Me."

"We."

"Look . . ."

Only the slight reflection of the light from her pupils showed that her eyes were open and looking at me. "Who do you belong to, Mike?"

"You tell me."

She didn't answer. Her eyes opened halfway and there was something sad in the way her lips tried to curve into a smile. I said, "All right, kid, you know the answer. It's we and if I stick my neck out you can be there to help me get back in time." I picked the .45 up off the floor beside the chair, slid the clip out and thumbed the shells into my palm. "Your boy Mike is getting on in years, pal. Soft maybe?"

There was laughter in the sad smile now. "Not soft. Smarter. We're up against something that's so big pure muscle won't even dent it. We're up against a big brain and being smart is the only thing that's going to move it. At least you have the sense to change your style."

"Yeah."

"It won't be so easy."

"I know. I'm not built that way." I grinned at her. "Let's not worry about it. Everybody's trying to step on me because they don't want me around. Some of 'em got different reasons, but the big one is they're afraid I'll spoil their play. That happened before too. Let's make it happen again."

Velda said, "But let's not try so hard, huh? Seven years is a long time to wait for a guy." Her teeth were a white flash in the middle of her smile. "I'd like him in good shape when he gets ready to take the jump."

I said, "Yeah," but not so loud that she heard me.

"Where do we take it from here, Mike?"

I let the shells dribble from my fingers into the ash tray. They lay there, deadly and gleaming, but helpless without the mother that could give them birth.

"Berga Torn," I said. "We'll start with her. I want those sanitarium records. I want her life history and the history of anybody she was associated

53

with. That's your job."

"And you?" she asked.

"Evello. Carl Evello. Someplace he comes into this thing and he's my job."

Velda nodded, drummed her fingernails against the arm of the chair and stared across the room. "He won't be easy."

"Nobody's easy."

"Especially Evello. He's organized. While you were under wraps in the hospital I saw a few people who had a little inside information on Evello. There wasn't much and what there was of it was mostly speculation, but it put the finger on a theme you might be interested in."

"Such as?"

She looked at me with a half smile, a beautiful jungle animal sizing up her mate before telling him what was outside the mouth of the den. "Mafia," she said.

I could feel it starting way down at my toes, a cold, burning flush that crept up my body and left in its wake a tingling sensation of rage and fear that was pure emotion and nothing else. It pounded in my ears and dried my throat until the words that came out were scratchy, raspy sounds that didn't seem to be part of me at all.

"How did they know?"

"They don't. They suspect, that's all. The Federal agencies are interested in the angle."

"Yeah," I said. "They *would* be interested. They'd go in on their toes, too. No wonder they don't want me fishing around."

"You make too much noise."

"Things happen, don't they?"

Velda didn't answer that one either.

"So now it makes sense," I told her. "They have the idea I'm in the deal someplace but they can't come out and say it. They play twenty questions hoping I do have a share of it so they'll have someplace to start. They won't give up until the day they die or I do because once the finger touches you it never comes away. There's no such thing as innocence, just innocence touched with guilt is as good a deal as you can get."

Velda's mouth moved slowly. "Maybe it's a good thing, Mike. It's a funny world. Pure innocence as such doesn't enter in much nowadays. There's always at least one thing people try to hide." She paused and ran her finger along the side of her cheek. "If a murderer is hung for the wrong killing, who is wrong?"

"That's a new twist for you, kid."

"I got it from you."

"Then finish it."

Her fingers reached out and plucked a cigarette from the pack. It was a graceful, feminine motion that spoke of soft girlishness, the texture of her skin satiny and amber in the light. You could follow the fingers into the hand and the hand into the arm, watching the curves melt into each other like a beautiful painting. Just watching like that and you could forget the two times that same hand held a snarling, spitting rod that chewed a guy's guts out. "Now innocence touched with guilt pays off," she said. "You'll be one of the baited hooks they'll use until something bites."

"And in the end the public will benefit."

"That's right." She grinned, the corner of her mouth twisting upward a little. "But don't feel badly about it, Mike. They're stealing your stuff. You taught them that trick a long time ago."

My fingers went out and began to play with the slugs that squatted in the bottom of the ash tray where I had dropped them. She watched me from across the room, her eyes half closed in speculation. Then she uncurled, tossed my deck of smokes into the chair beside me and reached for her coat.

I didn't watch her walk away. I sat there dreaming of the things I'd like to do and how maybe if nobody was there to see me I'd do anyway. I was dreaming of a lot of fat faces with jowls that got big and loose on other people's meat and how they'd look with that smashed, sticky expression that comes with catching the butt end of a .45 across their noses. I was dreaming of a slimy foreign secret army that held a parade of terror under the Mafia label and laughed at us with our laws and regulations and how fast their damned smug expressions would change when they saw the fresh corpses of their own kind day after day.

She didn't have to go far to read my mind. She had seen me look like this before. She didn't have to go far to get me back on the track, either. "Isn't it about time you taught them some fresh tricks, Mike?" Velda said softly.

Then she left and the room got a little darker.

56

Chapter Five

I sat there for a while, staring at the multicolored reflections of the city that made my window a living, moving kaleidoscope. The voice of the monster outside the glass was a constant drone, but when you listened long enough it became a flat, sarcastic sneer that pushed ten million people into bigger and better troubles, and then the sneer was heard for what it was, a derisive laugh that thought blood running from an open wound was funny, and death was the biggest joke of all.

Yeah, it laughed at people like me and you. It was the voice of the guy with the whip who laughed at each stroke to drown out the screams of the victim. A subtle voice that hid small cries, a louder voice that covered the anguished moans.

I sat and heard it and thought about it while the statistics ran through my head. So many a minute killed by cars, so many injured. So many dead an hour by out-and-out violence. So many this and so many that. It made a long impressive list that was recited at board meetings and assemblies.

There was only one thing left out. How many were scared stiff? How many lay awake nights worrying about things they shouldn't have to worry about at all? How many wondered where their kids were and what they were doing. *How many knew the army of silent men who made their whispered demands and either got them or extracted payment according to the code?*

Then I knew the voice outside for what it was. Not some intangible monster after all. Not some gigantic mechanical contrivance that could act of its own accord. Not a separate living being with its own rules and decrees. Not one of those things.

People, that's all.

Just soft, pulpy people, most of them nice. And some of them filthy and twisted who gorged themselves on flesh and puffed up with the power they had so that when they got stuck they popped like ripe melons and splashed their guts all over the ground.

The Mafia. The stinking, slimy Mafia. An oversize mob of ignorant, lunkheaded jerks who ruled with fear and got away with it because they had money to back themselves up.

The Black Hand? You think you can laugh it off? You think all that stuff went out with prohibition? There's a lot of widows around who can tell you differently. Widowers, too.

Like Velda said, it wasn't going to be easy at all. You don't just ask around where you can find the top boy.

First you find somebody to ask and if you're not dead by then, or he's not dead, you ask. Then you ask and look some more, each time coming closer to the second when a bullet or a knife reaches across space and spears you.

There's a code they work by, a fixed unbreakable code. Once the Mafia touches you it never takes its hand away. And if you make one move, just one single, hesitant move to get out from under, it's all over. Sometimes it takes a day or two, even a year maybe, but it was all over from then.

You get dead.

In a sense though, it was funny. Someplace at the top of the heap was a person. From him the fear radiated like from the center of a spiderweb. He sat on his throne and made a motion of his hand and somebody died. He made another motion and somebody was twisted until they screamed. A nod of his head did something that sent a guy leaping from a roof because he couldn't take it any more.

Just one person did that. One soft, pulpy person.

I started to grin a little bit thinking how he'd act stripped of weapons and his power for a minute or so in a closed room with someone who didn't like him. I could almost see his face behind the glass and my grin got bigger because I was pretty sure of what I was going to do now.

It was late, but only by the clock. The city was yawning and stretching after its supper, waking up to start living. The rain had died, leaving a low grumble in the skies overhead to announce its passing. The air was fresher now, the light a little brighter, and the parade of cabs had slowed

59

down enough so I could whistle one down and hop a ride over to Pat's apartment.

He let me in with a grin and muttered something between the folder of papers he had clamped in his teeth, waved me into the living room and took my coat. His eyes made a casual sweep over my chest and he didn't have to look a second time to tell I wasn't wearing a rig under my arm.

Pat said, "Drink?"

"Not now."

"It's only ginger ale."

I shook my head and sat down. He filled his glass, relaxed into a wing chair and shoved all the papers into an envelope. "Glad to see you traveling light."

"Didn't you expect me to?"

His mouth crooked up at the corner. "I figured you'd know better than not to. Just don't blame me for the deal, that's all."

"You're not too sorry about it, are you?"

"As a matter of fact, no." His fingers tapped the envelope, then his eyes came up to mine. "It puts you on the spot as far as business is concerned, but I don't imagine you'll starve."

"I don't imagine I will either," I grinned back at him. "How long am I supposed to be in solitary for?"

He didn't like the grin at all. He got those wrinkles around his eyes that showed when something was getting under his hide and took a long drag on the drink to muffle what he knew I saw. "When they're ready to lift it they'll lift it and not before."

"They won't have it that soft," I told him.
"No?"

I flicked a butt into my mouth and lit it. "To-morrow you can remind 'em I'm an incorporated business, a taxpayer and a boy with connections. My lawyer has a judge probably getting up a show cause right now and until they settle the case in court they aren't pulling any bill-of-attainder stuff on me."

"You got a mouthful of words on that one, Mike."

"Uh-huh. And you know what I'm talking about. Nobody, not even a Federal agency is going to pull my tail and not get chewed a little bit."

His hands got too tight around the glass. "Mike . . . this isn't just murder."

"I know."

"How much?"

"No more than before. I've been thinking around it though."

"Any conclusions?"

"One." I looked at him, hard. "Mafia."

Nothing changed in his face. "So?"

"I can be useful if you'd quit booting me around." I took a drag on the smoke and let it curl out into the light. "I don't have to pull my record out. You know it as well as I do. Maybe I have shot up a few guys, but the public doesn't seem to miss them any. If your buddies think I'm stupid enough to go busting in on something over my head without knowing what I'm doing then it's time they took a refresher course. They haven't got one guy in Washington that's smarter than I am . . . not one guy. If they had they'd be making more moolah than I am and don't fool yourself thinking they're in there for love of the job. It's about the limit they can do."

"You sure think a lot of yourself."

"I have to, friend. Nobody else does. Besides, I'm still around when a lot of others have taken their last car ride."

Pat finished off the glass and swirled the last few drops around the bottom. "Mike," he said, "if I had my way I'd have you and ten thousand more in on this thing. That's about how many we'd need to fight it. As it is, I'm a city cop and I take orders. What do you want from me?"

"You say it, Pat."

He laughed this time. It was like the old days when neither one of us gave a damn about anything and if we had to hate it was the same thing. "Okay, you want me for your third arm. You're going to dive into this thing no matter who says what and as long as you are we'd might as well use your talents instead of tripping over them."

The grin was real. It was six years ago and not now any longer. The light was back in his eyes again and we were a team riding over anything that stood in our way. "Now I'll tell you something, Mike," he said, "I don't like the way the gold-badge boys do business either. I don't like political meddling in crime and I'm sick of the stuff that's been going on for so long. Everybody is afraid to move and it's about time something jolted them. For so damn long I've been listening to people say that this racket is over our heads that I almost began to believe it myself. Okay, I'll lay my job on the line. Let's give it a spin and see what happens. Tell me what you want and I'll feed it to you. Just don't hash up the play . . . at least not for a while yet. If something good comes of it I'll have a talking point and maybe I can keep my job."

"I can always use a partner."

"Thanks. Now let's hear your angle."

"Information. Detailed."

He didn't have to go far for it. The stuff was right there in his lap. He pulled it all out of the envelope and thumbed the sheets apart. The light behind his head made the sheets translucent enough so the lines of type stood out and there weren't very many lines.

"Known criminals with Mafia connections," he drawled. "Case histories of Mafia efficiency and police negligence. Twenty pages of arrests with hardly enough convictions to bother about. Twenty pages of murder, theft, dope pushing, and assorted felonies and all we're working with are the bottom rungs of the ladder. We can name some of the big ones but don't fool yourself and think they are the top joes. The boys up high don't have names we know about."

"Is Carl Evello there?"

Pat looked at the sheets again and threw them on the floor in disgust. "Evello isn't anywhere. He's got one of those investigatable incomes but it looks like he'll be able to talk his way out of it."

"Berga Torn?"

"Now we're back to murder. One of many."

"We don't think alike there, Pat."

"No?"

"Berga was special. She was so special they put a crew of boys on her who knew their business. They don't do that for everybody. Why did the committee want her?"

I could see him hesitate a moment, shrug and make up his mind. "There wasn't much to the Torn dame. She was a good-looking head with a respectable mind but engaged in a mucky racket, if you get what I mean."

"I know."

"There was a rumor that Evello was keeping her for a while. It was during the time he was raking in a pile. The same rumor had he gave her the boot and the committee figured she'd be mad enough to spill what she knew about him."

"Evello wouldn't be that dumb," I said.

"When it comes to dames, guys can be awfully dumb," he grinned at me knowingly.

"Finish it."

"The feds approached her. She was scared stiff, but she indicated that there was something she could give out, but she wanted time to collect her information and protection after she let it out."

"Great." I snuffed the butt out and leaned back in the chair. "I can see Washington assigning her a permanent bodyguard."

"She was going to appear before the committee masked."

"No good. Evello could still spot her from the info she handed them."

Pat confirmed the thought with a nod. "In the meantime," he went on, "she got the jitters. Twice she got away from the men assigned to cover her. Before the month was out she was practically hysterical and went to a doctor. He had her committed to a sanitarium and she was supposed to stay there for three weeks. The investigation was held up, there were agents assigned to guard the sanitarium, she got away and was killed."

"Just like that."

"Just like that only you were there when it happened."

"Nice of me."

"That's what those Washington boys thought."

"Coincidence is out," I said.

"Naturally." His mouth twitched again. "They don't know that you're the guy things happen to. Some people are accident prone. You're coincidence prone."

"I've thought of it that way," I told him. "Now what about the details of her escape?"

He shrugged and shook his head slightly. "Utter simplicity. The kind of thing you can't beat. Precautions were taken for every inconceivable thing and she does the conceivable. She picked up a raincoat and shoes from the nurses' quarters and walked out the main entrance with two female attendants. It was raining at the time and one of them had an umbrella and they stayed together under it the way women will who try to keep their hair dry or something. They went as far as the corner together, the other two got in a bus while she kept on walking."

"Wasn't a pass required at the gate?"

He nodded deeply, a motion touched with sarcasm. "Sure, there was a pass all right, each of the two had a pass and showed it. Maybe the guy thought he saw the third one. At least he said he thought so."

"I suppose somebody was outside the gate too?"

"That's right. Two men, one on foot and one in a car. Neither had seen the Torn girl and were there to stop anyone making an unauthorized exit."

I let out a short grunt.

Pat said, "They thought it *was* authorized, Mike."

I laughed again. "That's what I mean. *They thought*. Those guys are supposed to think right or not at all. Those are the guys who had my ticket lifted. Those are the guys who want no interference. Nuts."

"Anyway, she got away. That's it."

"Okay, we'll leave it there. What attitude are the cops taking?"

"It's murder so they're working it from that end."

"And getting nowhere," I added.

"So far," Pat said belligerently. I grinned at him and the scowl that creased his forehead disappeared. "Lay off. How do you plan to work it?"

"Where's Evello?"

"Right here in the city."

"And the known Mafia connections?"

Pat looked thoughtful a moment. "Other big cities, but their operational center is here too." He bared his teeth in a tight grimace. His eyes went hard and nasty as he said, "Which brings us to the end of our informative little discussion about the Mafia. We know who some of them are and how they operate, but that's as far as it goes."

"Washington doesn't have anything?"

"Sure, but what good does it do. Nobody fingers the Mafia. There's that small but important little item known as evidence."

"We'll get it," I told him, ". . . one way or another. It's still a big organization. They need capital to operate."

Pat stared at me like he would a kid. "Sure, just like that. You know how they raise that capital? They squeeze it out of the little guy. It's an extra tax he has to pay. They put the bite on guys who are afraid to talk or who can't talk. They run an import business that drives the Narcotics Division nuts. They got their hand in every racket that exists with a political cover so heavy you can't bust through it with a sledge hammer."

He didn't have to remind me. I knew how they operated. I said, "Maybe, chum, maybe. Could be that nobody's really tried hard enough yet."

He grunted something under his breath, then,

"You still didn't say how you were going to work it."

I pushed myself out of the chair, wiping my hand across my face. "First Berga Torn. I want to find out more about her."

Pat reached down and picked the top sheet off the pile he had dropped on the floor beside him. "You might as well have this then. It's as much as anyone has to start with."

I folded it up and stuck it in my pocket without looking at it. "You'll let me know if anything comes up?"

"I'll let you know." I picked up my coat and started for the door.

"And Mike . . ."

"Yeah?"

"This is a two-way deal, remember?"

"Yeah, I remember."

Downstairs, I stood in front of the building a minute. I took the time to stick a Lucky in my mouth and even more time lighting it. I let the flare of the match bounce off my face for a good ten seconds, then dragged in deeply on the smoke and whipped it back into the night air. The guy in the doorway of the apartment across the streeted stirred and made a hesitant motion of having come out of the door and not knowing which way to walk. I turned east and he made up his mind. He turned east too.

Halfway down the block I crossed over to make it a little easier on him. Washington didn't discount

68

shoe leather as expenses so there was no sense giving the boy a hard time. I went three more blocks closer to the subway station and pulled a few gimmicks that had him practically climbing up my back.

This time I had a good look at him and was going to say hello to add insult to injury when I caught the end of a gun muzzle in my ribs and knew he wasn't Washington at all.

He was young and good-looking until he smiled, then the crooked march of short, stained teeth across his mouth made him an expensively dressed punk on a high-class job. There was no hop behind his pupils so he was a classy workman being paid by an employer who knew what the score was. The teeth smiled bigger and he started to tell me something when I ripped his coat open and the gun in the pocket wasn't pointing at me any more. He was half spun around fighting to get the rod loose as the side of my hand caught him across the neck and he sat down on the sidewalk with his feet out in front of him, plenty alive, plenty awake, but not even a little bit active.

I picked the Banker's Special out of his hand, broke it, dumped the shells into the gutter and tossed the rod back into his lap. His eyes were hurting. They were all watered up like he was ashamed of himself.

"Tell your boss to send a man out on the job the next time," I said.

I walked on down the street and turned into the subway kiosk wondering what the deuce had happened to Washington. Little boy blue back on the sidewalk would have a good story to take home to papa this time. Most likely he wouldn't get his allowance. At least they'd know a pro was in the game for a change.

I shoved a dime in the turnstile, went through, pulled the sheet out of my pocket, glanced at it once and walked over to the downtown platform.

Chapter Six

Something happens to Brooklyn at night. It isn't a sister borough any more. She withdraws to herself and pulls the shades down, then begins a life that might seem foreign to an outsider. She's strange, exciting, tinted with bright lights, yet elusive somehow.

I got off the Brighton Line at De Kalb and went up to the street. A guy on the corner pointed the way to the address I wanted and I walked the few blocks to it.

What I was looking for was an old-fashioned brownstone, a hangover from a half-century past that had the number painted on the door and looked at the street with dull, blank eyes. I went up the four sandstone steps, held a match to the mailboxes and found what I wanted.

The names CARVER and TORN were there, but somebody had drawn a pencil through the two of them and had written in BERNSTEIN underneath. All I could do was mutter a little under my breath and punch the end button on the line, the one labeled SUPER. I leaned on it until the door started clicking then I opened it and went in.

He came to the door and I could almost see his face. Part of it stuck out behind the fleshy shoulder of a woman who towered all around him and glared at me as if I had crawled up out of a hole. Her hair was a gray mop gathered into tiny knots and clamped in place with metal curlers. She bulged through the bathrobe, trying to slow down her breathing enough so she could say something. Her hands were big and red, the knuckles showing as they bit into her hips.

Dames. The guy behind her looked scared to death. She said, "What the hell do you want! You know what time it is? You think . . ."

"Shut up." Her mouth stopped. I leaned against the door jamb. "I'm looking for the super."

"I'm the . . ."

"You're not anything to me, lady. Tell your boy to come out." I thought her face would fall apart. "Tell him," I repeated.

When men learn to be men maybe they can handle dames. There was something simpering in the way she forced a smile and stepped aside.

The boy didn't want to come out, but he did. He made himself as big as he could without it helping much. "Yes?"

I showed him the badge I still had. It didn't mean a thing any more, but it still shined in the light and wasn't something everybody carried. "Get your keys."

"Yessir, yessir." He reached up beside the door, unhooked a ring and stepped back into the hall.

72

The dame said, "You wait a minute, I'll be right . . ."

He seemed to stand on his toes. "*You* wait right there until I come *back*," he told her. "*I'm* the super." He turned and grinned at me. Behind him his wife's face puffed out and the door slammed.

"Yessir?" he said.

"Berga Torn's place. I want to go through it."

"But the police have already been through there."

"I know."

"Today I rented it already."

"Anybody there now?"

"Not yet. Tomorrow they're supposed to come."

"Then let's go."

First he hesitated, then he shrugged and started up the stairs. Two flights up he fitted a key into the lock of a door and threw it open. He felt around for the light switch, flipped it and stood aside for me.

I don't know what I expected to find. Maybe it was more curiosity than anything that dragged me up there. The place had been gone over by experts and if anything had been worth taking it was gone by now. It was what you might call a functional apartment and nothing more. The kitchen and living room were combined with a bathroom sandwiched between two bedrooms that jutted off the one wall. There was enough furniture to be comfortable, nothing gaudy and nothing out of place.

"Whose stuff is this?"

"We rent furnished. What you see belongs to the landlord."

I walked into the bedroom and opened the door of the closet. A half dozen dresses and a suit hung there. The floor was lined with shoes. The dresser was the same way, filled to the brim. The clothes were good, fairly new, but not the type that came out of exclusive shops.

Stockings were neatly rolled up and packed into a top drawer. Beside them were four envelopes, two with paid-up receipts, one a letter from the Millburn Steamship Line saying that there were no available berths on the liner Cedric and how sorry they were, and the other a heavier envelope holding about a dozen Indianhead pennies.

The other small drawer was cluttered with half-used lipsticks and all the usual junk a dame can collect in hardly any time at all.

It was the other bedroom that gave me the surprise. There was nothing there at all. Just a made-up bed, a cleaned-out closet and dresser drawers lined with old sheets of newspaper.

The super watched me until I backed out into the living room, saying nothing.

"Whose room?" I jerked my thumb at the empty place.

"Miss Carver's."

"Where is she?"

"Two days ago . . . she moved out."

"The police see her?"

He nodded, a fast snap of the head. "Maybe

that's why she moved out."

"You going to empty this place out?"

"Guess I got to. The lease is up next month, but it was paid in advance. Hope I don't get in trouble renting so soon."

"Who paid it?"

"Torn's name is on the lease." He looked at me pointedly.

"I didn't ask that."

"She handed me the dough." I stared at him hard and he fumbled with his pajamas again. "How many times do I have to tell you guys. I don't know where she got the dough. Far as I know she didn't do any messing around. This place sure wasn't no office or that nosy old lady of mine would've known about it."

"Did she have any men here to see her?"

"Mister," he said, "there's twelve apartments in this rattrap and I can't keep track of who comes in and who goes out so long as they're paid up. If you ask me right off I'd say she wasn't no tramp. She was a dame splitting her quarters with another dame who paid her dough and didn't make trouble. If a guy was keeping her he sure didn't get his money's worth. If you want to know what I think then I'd say yes, she was being kept. Maybe the both of 'em. The old lady never thought so or she would've given them the boot, that's for sure."

"Okay then," I said, "that's it."

He held the door open for me. "You think anything's going to come of this?"

"Plenty."

The guy was another lip licker. "There won't be . . ."

"Don't worry about it. You know how I can reach the Carver girl?"

The look he gave me was quick and worried. "She didn't leave no address."

I made it sound very flat and businesslike. "You know . . . when you step in front of the law there's charges that can be pressed."

"Aw, look, mister, if I knew . . ." His tongue came out and passed over his mouth again. He thought about it, shrugged, then said, "Okay. Just don't let my wife know. She called today. She's expecting some mail from her boy friend and asked me to send it to her." He pulled in a deep breath and let it out in a sigh. "She don't want anybody to know where she is. Got a pencil?"

I handed him one with the remains of an envelope and he jotted it down.

"Wish I could do something right for a change. The kid sounded pretty worried."

"You don't want to buck the law, do you friend?"

"Guess not."

"Okay, then you did right. Tell you what though . . . don't bother giving it out to anyone else. I'll see her, but she won't know how I reached her. How's that?"

His face showed some relief. "Swell."

"By the way," I said, "what was she like?"

"Carver?"

"Yeah."

"Kind of a pretty blonde. Hair like snow."

"I'll find her," I said.

The number was on Atlantic Avenue. It was the third floor over a secondhand store and there was nothing to guide you in but the smell. All the doorbells had names that had been there long enough to get dirtied up, but the newest one said TRENTEN when it didn't mean that at all.

I punched the button three times while I stood there in the dark, heard nothing ringing so I eased myself into the smell. It wasn't just an odor. It was something that moved, something warm and fluid that came down the stairs, tumbling over slowly, merging with other smells until it leaked out into the street.

In each flight there were fourteen steps, a landing, a short corridor that took you to the next flight and at the top of the last one, a door. Up there the smell was different. It wasn't any fresher; it just smelled better. A pencil line of light marked the sill and for a change there was no bag of garbage to trip over.

I rapped on the door and waited. I did it again and springs creaked inside. A quiet little voice said, "Yes?"

"Carver?"

Again, "Yes." A bit tired-sounding this time.

"I'd like to speak to you. I'm pushing my card through under the door."

"Never mind. Just come right in."

I felt for the knob, twisted it and pushed the door open.

She was sitting there swallowed up in a big chair facing me, the gun in her hand resting on her knee in a lazy fashion and there wasn't even the slightest bit of doubt that it would start going off the second I breathed too hard.

Carver wasn't pretty. She was small and full bodied, but she wasn't pretty. Maybe no dame can be pretty with a rod in her mitt, even one with bleached white hair and a scarlet mouth. A black velvet robe outlined her against the chair, seeming like the space of nighttime between the white of her hair and that of the fur-lined slippers she wore.

For a minute she looked at me, her eyes wandering over me slowly. I let her look and pushed the door shut. Maybe she was satisfied by what she saw, maybe not. She didn't say anything, but she didn't put the gun away either. I said, "Expecting someone else?"

What she did with her mouth didn't make up a smile. "I don't know. What have you to say?"

"I'll say what it takes to make you point that heater someplace else."

"You can't talk that loud or that long, friend."

"Do I reach in my pocket for a smoke?"

"There's some on the table beside you. Use those."

I picked one up, almost went for my lighter in my pocket, thought better of it and took the matches that went with the cigarettes. "You're sure not good company, kid." I blew a stream of smoke at the floor and rocked on my toes. That little round hole in the tip of the automatic never came off my stomach.

"The name is Mike Hammer," I told her. "I'm a private investigator. I was with Berga Torn when she got knocked off."

This time the rod moved. I was looking right down the barrel.

"More," her mouth said.

"She was trying to hitch a ride to the city. I picked her up, ran a roadblock that was checking for her, got edged off the road by a car and damn near brained by a pack of hoods who were playing for keeps. I was there with my head dented in when they worked her over and behind the wheel of the car they pushed over the cliff. To them I was a handy, class-A red herring that was supposed to cover the real cause of her death only it didn't quite happen that way."

"How did it happen?"

"I was thrown clear. If you want I'll show you my scars."

"Never mind."

So we stared at each other for a longer minute and I was still looking down the barrel and the hole kept getting bigger and bigger.

"You loaded?"

"The cops lifted my rod and P.I. ticket."

"Why?"

"Because they knew I'd bust into this thing and they wanted to keep me out."

"How did you find me?"

"It's not hard to find people when you know how. Anybody could do it." Her eyes widened momentarily, seemed to deepen, then narrowed sharply.

"Suppose I don't believe you," she said.

I sucked in a lungful of smoke and dropped the butt to the floor. I didn't bother to squash it out. I let it lie there until you could smell the stink of burned wool in the room and felt my face start to tighten around the edges. I said, "Kid, I'm sick of answering questions. I'm sick of having guns pointed at me. You make the second tonight and if you don't stow that thing I'm going to beat the hell out of you. What'll it be?"

I didn't scare her. The gun came down until it rested in her lap and for the first time the stiffness left her face. Carver just looked tired. Tired and resigned. The scarlet slash of her mouth made a wry grimace of sadness. "All right," she said, "sit down."

So I sat down. No matter what else I could have done, nothing would have been more effective. The bewilderment showed on her face, the way her body arched before sinking back again. Her leg moved and the gun dropped to the floor and stayed there.

"Aren't you . . ."

"Who were you expecting, Carver?"

"The name is Lily." Her tongue was a lighter pink against the scarlet as it swept across her lips.

"Who, Lily?"

"Just . . . men." Her eyes were hopeful now. "You . . . told me the truth?"

"I'm not one of them if that's what you mean. Why did they come?"

The hardness left her face. It seemed to melt away like a film that should never have been there and now she was pretty. Her hair was a pile of snow that reflected the loveliness of her face. She breathed heavily, the robe drawing tight at regular intervals.

"They wanted Berga."

"Let's start at the beginning. With you and Berga. How's that?"

Lily paused and stared into the past. "Before the war, that's when we met. We were dance-hall hostesses. It was the first night for the both of us and we both sort of stuck together. A week later we found an apartment and shared it."

"How long?"

"About a year. When the war came I was pretty sick of things and went into a defense plant. Berga quit too . . . but what she did for a living was her business. She was a pretty good kid. When I was sick she moved back in and took care of me. After the war I lost my job when the plant closed down and she got a friend of hers to get me a job in a night club in Jersey."

"Did she work there too?" I asked.

The white hair made a negative. "She was . . . doing a lot of things."

"Anybody special?"

"I don't know. I didn't ask. We went back living in the same apartment for a while, though she was paying most of the bills. She seemed to have a pretty good income."

Lily's eyes came off the wall behind my head and fastened on mine. "That's when I noticed her starting to change."

"How?"

"She was . . . scared."

"Did she say why?"

"No. She laughed it off. Twice she booked passage to Europe, but couldn't get the ship she wanted and didn't go."

"She was that scared."

Lily shrugged, saying nothing, saying much. "It seemed to grow on her. Finally she wouldn't even leave the house at all. She said she didn't feel well, but I knew she was lying."

"When was this?"

"Not so very long ago. I don't remember just when."

"It doesn't matter."

"She went out once in a while after that. Like to the movies or for groceries. Never very far. Then the police came around."

"What did they want?"

"Her."

"Questions or an arrest?"

"Questions, mostly. They asked me some things too. Nothing I knew about. That night I saw someone following me home." Her face had a curious strained look about it. "It's been that way every night since. I don't know if they've found me here yet or not."

"Cops?"

"Not cops." She said it very simply, very calmly, but couldn't quite hide the terror that tried to scream the answer out.

She begged me to say something, but I let her squeeze it out herself. "The police came again, but Berga wouldn't tell them anything." The tongue moistened the lips again. The scarlet was starting to wash away and I could see the natural tones of the wet flesh. "The other men came . . . they were different from the police. Federal men, I think. They took her away. Before she came back . . . *Those* men came."

She put something into the last three words that wasn't in the others, some breathless, nameless fear. Her hands were tight balls with the nails biting into the palms. A glassiness had passed over her eyes while she thought about it, then vanished as if afraid it had been seen.

"They said I'd die if I talked to anyone." Her hand moved up and covered her mouth. "I'm tired of being scared," she said. Her head drooped forward, nodding gently to the soft sobs that seemed to stick in her chest.

What's the answer? How do you tell them they won't die when they know you're lying about it because they're marked already?

I got up and walked to her chair, looked at her a second and sat down on the arm of it. I took her hand away from her face, tilted her chin up and ran my fingers through the snow piled on top of her head. It was as soft and as fine as it looked in the light and when my fingers touched her cheek

83

she smiled, dropped her eyes and let that beauty come through all the way, every bit of it that she had kept hidden so long. There was a faint smell of rubbing alcohol about her, a clean, pungent odor that seemed to separate itself from the perfume she wore.

Her eyes were big and dark, soft ovals under the delicate brows, her mouth full and pink, parted in the beginning of a smile. My fingers squeezed her shoulder easily and her head went back, the mouth parting even further and I bent down slowly.

"You won't die," I said.

And it was the wrong thing to say because the mouth that was so close to mine pulled back and everything had changed. I just sat there next to her for a little while until the dry sobs had stopped. There were no tears to be wiped away. Terror doesn't leave any tears. Not that kind of terror.

"What did they want to know about Berga?"

"I don't know," she whispered. "They made me tell everything I knew about her. They made me sit there while they went through her things."

"Did they find anything?"

"No. I . . . I don't think so. They were horribly mad about it."

"Did they hurt you?" I asked.

An almost imperceptible shudder went through her whole body. "I've been hurt worse." Her eyes drifted up to mine. "They were disgusting men. They'll kill me now, won't they?"

"If they do they've had it."

"But it would still be too late for me."

I nodded. It was all I could do. I got up, took the last smoke out of my old pack and tapped the butt against my knuckle. "Can't I take a look at that suitcase of hers?"

"It's in the bedroom." She pushed her hair back with a tired motion. "The closet."

I walked in, snapped on the light and found the closet. The suitcase was there where she said it was, a brown leather gladstone that had seen a lot of knocking around. I tossed it on the bed, unfastened the straps and opened it up.

But nothing was in there that could kill a person. Not unless a motive for murder was in a couple old picture albums, three yearbooks from high school, a collection of underwear, extra-short bathing suits, a stripper's outfit and a batch of old mail.

I thought maybe the mail would do it, but most of them were trivial answers from some friend to letters she had written and were postmarked from a hick town in Idaho. The rest were steamship folders and a tour guide of southern Europe. I shoved everything back in the suitcase, closed it up and dropped it in the closet.

When I turned around Lily was standing there in the doorway, a fresh cigarette in her mouth, one hand holding the robe closed around her waist, her hair a white cloud that seemed to hover above her. When she spoke the voice didn't sound as though it belonged to her at all.

"What am I to do now?"

I reached out and folded my hand over hers and drew her closer to me. The fingers were cold, her body was a warm thing that wanted to search for something.

"Got any place to go?"

"No," faintly.

"Money?"

"Just a little."

"Get dressed. How long will it take?"

"A . . . a few minutes."

For the briefest interval her face brightened with a new hope, then she smiled and shook her head. "It . . . won't do any good, I've seen men like that before. They're not like other people. They'd find me."

My laugh was short and hard. "We'll make it tough for them just the same. And don't kid yourself about them being too different. They're just like anybody else in most ways. They're afraid of things too. I'm not kidding you or me. You know what the score is so all we can do is give it a try."

I stopped for a second and let a thought run through my head again. I grinned down at her and said, "You know . . . don't be a bit surprised if you live a lot longer than you think you should."

"Why?"

"I have an idea the outfit who worked you over don't really know what they're after and they're not going to kill any leads until they get it."

"But I . . . don't have any idea . . ."

"Let them find that out for themselves," I interrupted. "Let's get you out of here as fast as we can."

I dropped her hand and pushed her into the bedroom. She looked at me, her face happy, then her body went tight and it showed in the way her eyes lit up, that crazy desire to say thanks somehow; but I pulled the door shut before she could do what she wanted to do and went inside opening a fresh deck of Luckies.

The gun was still there on the floor, a metallic glitter asleep on a bed of faded green wool. The safety was off and the hammer was still back. All that time in the beginning I was about a literal ounce away from being nice and dead. Lily Carver hadn't been fooling a bit.

She took almost five minutes. I heard the door open and turned around. It wasn't the same Lily. It was a new woman, a fresh and lovely woman who was a taller, graceful woman. It was one for whom the green gabardine suit had been intended, exquisitely molding every feature of her body. Her legs were silken things, their curves flashing enough to take your eyes away from the luxury of her hair that poked out under the hat.

It wasn't a worried or a scared Lily this time. It was a Lily who took my arm and held it tightly, smiling a smile that was real. "Where are we going, Mike?"

It was the first time she had said my name and I liked the way she said it.

"To my place," I told her.

We went downstairs and out on Atlantic Avenue.

We played a game of not being seen in case there were watchers and if there were they weren't good enough to keep up with us. We used the subway to go home and took a cab to the door. When I was sure nobody was in the lobby I took her in.

It was all very simple.

When we got upstairs I told her to hop into the sack and showed her the spare bedroom. She smiled, reached out and patted my cheek and said, "It's been a long time since I met a nice guy, Mike."

That strange excitement seemed to be inside her like a coiled spring. I squeezed her wrist and she knew what I was saying without having to use words and her mouth started to part.

I stopped it there.

Or maybe she stopped it.

The spring wound tighter and tighter, then I let her go and walked away.

Behind me the door closed softly and I thought I heard a whispered "Good night, Mike."

I started it that night. At three-thirty the word went out in the back room of a gin mill off Forty-second and Third. Before morning it would yell and before the night came again it would pay off. One way or another.

Wherever they were, whoever they were, they would hear about it. They'd know me and know what the word meant. They'd sit and think for a little while and if they knew me well enough maybe they'd feel a little bit sweaty and not so sure of themselves any more. They couldn't laugh it off. With anybody else, perhaps, but not with me.

Wise guys. A pack of conniving slobs with the world in their hands and the power and money to buck a government while they sat on their fat tails, yet before morning there wouldn't be one of them who didn't have a funny feeling around his gut.

This time they had to move.

The word was out.

I went back to the apartment and listened at the door of Lily's room. I could hear her regular, heavy breathing. I stood there a minute, took a final drag on the butt, put it out and headed for my sack.

Chapter Seven

She was up when the phone rang in the morning. I heard the dishes rattling and smelt the coffee. She called out, "Any time you're ready, come eat."

I said okay and picked up the phone.

The voice was low and soft, the kind you'd never miss in a million years. It was the best way to wake up and it showed in my voice when I said, "Hi Velda, what's doing?"

"Plenty is doing, but nothing I want to talk about over the phone."

"Get something?"

"Yes."

"Where are you now?"

"Down at the office. A place you ought to try to get to once a week, at least."

"You know how things are, honey," I said.

Lily looked in the door, waved and pointed toward the kitchen. I nodded, glad that Velda didn't know how things were right then.

"Where were *you* last night? I called until I was too tired to stay awake and tried again this morning."

"I was busy."

"Oh, Pat called." She tried to keep her voice its natural huskiness but it wanted to get away.

"I suppose he said too much."

"He said enough." She stopped and I could hear her breathing into the phone. "Mike, I'm scared."

"Well don't be, kitten. I know what I'm doing. You ought to know that."

"I'm still scared. I think somebody tried to break into my apartment last night."

That one got a low whistle out of me. "What happened?"

"Nothing. I heard a noise in the lock for a while but whoever was trying it gave up. I'm glad I got that special job now. Are you coming over?"

"Not right away."

"You ought to. A lot of mail is piling up. I paid all the bills, but you have a sackful of personal stuff."

"I'll get to it later. Look, did you make out on that info?"

"Somewhat. Do you want it now?"

"*Right* now, kitten. I'll meet you in the Texan Bar in an hour."

"All right, Mike."

"And kitten . . . you got that little heater of yours handy?"

"Well . . ."

"Then keep it handy but don't let it show."

"It's handy."

"Good. Grab a cab and get over there."

"I'll be there in an hour."

I slapped the phone back, hopped up and took

91

a fast shower. Lily had everything on the table when I got there, a hopeful smile on her face. The table was spread with enough for a couple of lumberjacks and I ate until I made a dent in the mess, then went for seconds on the coffee.

Lily handed me a fresh pack of Luckies, held out a match and smiled again when I slumped back in my chair. "Have enough?"

"Are you kidding? I'm a city boy, remember?"

"You don't look like a city boy."

"What do I look like?"

Her eyes did it slow. Up and down twice, then a steady scrutiny of my face. For a minute it was supposed to be funny, but the second time there was no humor in it. The eyes seemed to get bigger and deeper with some far-away hungry quality that was past defining. Then almost as quickly as it had come there was a crazy, fearful expression there in its place that lasted the blink of an eye and she forced a laugh out.

"You look like a nice guy, Mike. I haven't seen many nice guys. I'm afraid they make an impression."

"Don't get the wrong impression, Lily," I told her. "I used to think I wasn't much of a sentimentalist, but sometimes I wonder. Right now you're pretty important to me so I may look like a good egg to you. Just don't go walking off with anything while you're here or I'll look different to you."

Her smile got bigger. "You're not fooling me."

I tossed the butt in my empty cup and it fizzled

out. "So I'm getting old. You don't stay young in this racket very long."

"Mike . . ."

I knew what she was going to say before she said it. "I'll be gone for awhile. I don't know how long. The chances are nobody will be up here, but just to keep from sticking our necks out, don't answer that door. If a key goes in the lock it'll be me. Keep the chain on the door until I open it, look for yourself then to make sure and then open up."

"Supposing the phone rings?"

"Let it ring. If I want you I'll call the janitor, have him push the doorbell twice, then I'll call you. Got it?"

"I got it."

"Good. Now take it easy until I get back."

She gave me a slow, friendly wink and a grin, then followed it up with a soft kiss that formed on her lips and crossed the room to me. She was all dressed up with no place to go and didn't care, a beautiful white-headed doll with funny eyes that said she had been around too long and seen too many things. But now she looked happy.

I went downstairs, waited until a cab cruised by and grabbed it. We made the Texan Bar with ten minutes left out of the hour so I loafed around outside until a cab pulled into the curb and Velda got out.

Getting out of a cab is one of the things most women don't do right. But most women aren't Velda. Without half trying she made a production out of it. When you saw her do it you knew she wasn't getting out of a cab so much as making an entrance onto the street. Nothing showed, but there was so much to show that you had to watch to see if it would happen or not and even when it didn't you weren't a bit disappointed.

She turned around, gave me that impish grin and took my arm with a tight squeeze that said she was happy as all get out to see me and the guy with the packages beside me sighed and muttered something about some guys having all the luck.

Inside the Texan we picked a booth as far back as we could get, ordered up lunch for Velda, a beer for me and then she handed me the envelope from her handbag. "As much as I could get. It cost two hundred and a promise of favors to be repaid . . . if necessary."

"By you?"

Her face darkened, then twisted into a smile. "By you."

I slipped my finger under the flap and drew out the sheets. One was a handwritten copy of the sanitarium report with the rest filling in Berga Torn's life history. Velda had carried out instructions. At the bottom of the last page was a list of names.

Evello's was there. So was Congressman Geyfey's. At the tail end was Billy Mist and when I held my finger on it Velda said, "She went out with him periodically. She was seen with him, but whenever it was, the spotlight was on him . . . not her."

"No," I said softly, "the spotlight is always on Billy. The picture's starting to get dirty."

"Mike . . ." She was tapping her nails against the table. "Who is Billy Mist?"

I grunted, picked up a Lucky and lit it. "It's a picture that goes back pretty far. He used to be known as Billy the Kid and he had as many notches on his rod as the original, if they still notch rods. Just before the war he went legit. At least on the outside he looked clean. He's been tied into a lot of messy stuff but nothing's been proven against him."

"So?"

"He's a known Mafia connection," I said. "He sits pretty high, too."

Velda's face paled a little. "Brother!"

"Why?"

"Eddie Connely gave me the lead this morning in Toscio's Restaurant. He and another reporter seemed to have a pretty good inside track on the Torn gal, both of them being on the police beat. Trouble was, they had to suppress most of it and they were pretty disgusted. Anyway, Eddie mentioned Billy Mist and pointed him out. He was over at the bar and I turned around to look at him. About then he happened to turn around too, caught me watching him and got the wrong slant on things. He left his drink, came over and handed me the slimiest proposition I ever heard right out in the open. What I told him no lady should repeat, but Eddie and his pal got a little green and I thought the Mist character would pop his buttons.

Eddie didn't say much after that. He finished his coffee, paid the check and out they went."

I could feel my teeth showing through the grin. My chest was tight and things were happening in my head. Velda said, "Easy, chum."

I spit the cigarette out and didn't say anything for a minute. Billy Mist, the jerk with the duck's-tail haircut held down with a pound of grease. The tough guy who took what he wanted whenever he wanted. The uptown kid with the big money and the heavy connections.

When I got rid of the things in my head I squinted at her across the table. "Kitten, don't ever say I'm the guy who goes looking for trouble."

"Bad, Mike?"

"Bad enough. Mist isn't the type to forget. He can take anything except a slam at his manhood."

"I can take care of myself."

"Honey . . . *no* dame can take care of herself, including you. Be careful, will you?"

She seemed to smile all over. "Worried, Mike?"

"Certainly."

"Love me?"

"Yeah," I said, "I love you, but I go for the way you are and not the way you could look if Mist started working you over." I grinned at her and slapped my hand down over hers. "Okay, I'm not the romantic type this early and in this place."

"I don't care."

She sat there, tall and straight, the black page-boy hair swirling around her shoulders like a waterfall at night with the moon glinting on it.

Broad-shouldered, smooth and soft-looking, but firm underneath. She always had that hungry animal quality about her, eyes that drank everything in and when they looked at me seemed to drain me dry. Her mouth was expressive, with full, ripe lips that shone wetly, a crimson blossom that hid even white teeth.

I said it again and this time it sounded different and her fingers curled up over mine and squeezed.

A guy like me doesn't take the kind of look she was giving me very long. I shook my head, got my hand loose and went back to the report she had compiled.

"Let's not get off the track." Her laugh was a silent thing, but I knew she felt the same way I did. "We have three names here. What about the other three?"

Velda leaned across the table to see where I was pointing and I had to keep my eyes down. "Nicholas Raymond was an old flame apparently. She went with him before the war. He was killed in an auto accident."

It wasn't much, but to pick up details like that takes time. "Who said?"

"Pat. The police know that much about her."

"He's really going all out, isn't he?"

"The next one came from him too. Walter McGrath seemed to be another steady she was heavy on. He kept her for about a year during the war. She had an apartment on Riverside Drive then."

"He local?"

"No, from out of state, but he was in the city often."

"Business?"

"Lumber. Gray-market operations on steel too. He has a police record." She saw my eyebrows go up. "One income-tax evasion, two arrests for disorderly conduct, one conviction and suspended sentence for carrying concealed weapons."

"Where is he now?"

"He's been in the city here for about a month taking orders for lumber."

"Nice." She nodded agreement.

"Who's this Leopold Kawolsky?"

Velda frowned, her eyes turning a little darker. "I can't figure that one out. Eddie tapped him for me. Right after the war Berga was doing a number in a night club and when the place closed down there was a street brawl that seemed to center around her. This guy knocked off a couple of men giving her a hard time and a photog happened along who grabbed a pic for the front page of his tabloid. It was pure sensationalism, but the picture and the name stuck in Eddie's mind. The same thing happened about a month later and one of those kids who snap photos in the night clubs caught the action and submitted it for the usual pay-on-acceptance deal. That's how Eddie remembered who the girl was so well."

"The guy, honey . . . what about him?"

"I'm coming to him. From the pictures he looked like an ex-fighter. I called the sports editor of a magazine and he picked the name out for me. Kawolsky fought under the name Lee Kawolsky for a year and was looking pretty good until he broke his hand in training. After that he dropped out of the picture. Now, about a month and a half after the last public brawl Lee was hit by a truck and killed. Since there were two deaths by cars in the picture I went into the insurance records and went over them carefully. As far as I could tell, or anybody else for that matter, they were accidents, pure and simple."

"Pure and simple," I repeated. "The way it would have to look."

"I don't think so, Mike."

"Positive."

"Good enough." I ran my eyes over the copy of the medical report, folded it before I finished it and tucked it back into the envelope. "Brief me on this thing," I said.

"There really isn't much. She appeared before Dr. Martin Soberin for an examination, he diagnosed her case as extreme nervousness and suggested a rest cure. They mutually agreed on the sanitarium she was admitted to, an examination there confirmed Dr. Soberin's diagnosis and that was that. She was to stay there approximately four weeks. She paid in advance for her treatment."

If ever there was a mess, this was it. Everything out of place and out of focus. The ends didn't even try to meet. Meet? Hell, they were snarled up so completely nothing made any sense.

"How about this Congressman Geyfey?"

"Nothing special. He was seen with her at a

couple of political rallies. The man isn't married so he's clean that way. Frankly, I don't think he knew anything about her."

"This keeps getting worse."

"Don't get impatient. We're only getting started. What did Pat have to say about her?"

"It's all in writing. Probably the best parts they're not telling. Except for her connection with Evello she didn't seem to be out of the ordinary for a kid with her tastes. She was born in Pittsburgh in 1920. Her father was Swedish, her mother Italian. She made two trips to Europe, one when she was eight to Sweden, the next one in 1940 to Italy. The jobs she held didn't pay the kind of money she spent, but that's easy to arrange for a babe like that."

"Then Evello's the connection?"

"Evello's the one," I said. She looked at my face and her breathing seemed to get heavier. "He's here in New York. Pat'll give you the address."

"He's mine then?"

"Until I get around to him."

"What's the angle?"

"An approach. Better arrange for a regular introduction and let him do the rest. Find out who his friends are."

Only her eyes smiled. "Think I can pull it off?"

"You can't miss, baby, you can't miss."

The smile in her eyes got bigger.

"Where are you carrying the heater, kitten?"

The smile faded then. It got a little bit cold and deadly. "The shoulder rig. Left side and low down."

"Nobody'd ever notice, kitten."

"They're not supposed to," she said.

We finished eating and went back into the daylight. I watched her get into the cab the way she had got out and when the hack turned the corner I could feel the skin on my shoulder crawl thinking about where she was going. The next cab that came along I flagged down, gave him a Brooklyn address with instructions to stop by the Atlantic Avenue apartment first. The answer came fast enough when we reached the joint. The name was still on the wall but the neighbors said she had moved out during the night and the apartment was empty. A small truck with the trunks of a new customer started backing into the curb as we drove away.

The second Brooklyn address belonged to a newspaperman who had retired ten years ago. He was forty-nine years old but looked seventy. One side of his face had a scar that ran from the corner of his eye to his ear and down to his mouth. If he took off his shirt he could show you the three dimples in his stomach and the three larger angry pink scars in his back. One arm couldn't move at the elbow. He hadn't retired because he had wanted to. Seems like he had written an exposé about the Mafia one time.

When I came out it was two hours later and I had a folio of stuff under my arm that would have been worth ten grand to any good slick magazine. I got it free. I took another cab back uptown, sat in the back room of a drug store a buddy of mine ran, went through it twice, then wrapped it and mailed it back to the guy I got it from. I went into a bar and had a beer while the facts settled down in my mind. While I sat there I tried to keep from looking at myself in the mirror behind the back bar but it didn't work. My face wasn't pretty at all. Not at all. So I moved to a booth in the back that had no mirrors.

Evello's name was there. Billy Mist's name was there. In the very beginning. They were punks then but they showed promise. The guy in Brooklyn said you didn't pick up the connections any more because most likely the boys had new assignments. They had been promoted. That was a long time ago so by now they should be kings. There were other names that I didn't know, but before long I'd know. There were empty spaces where names should be but couldn't be supplied and those were in the throne room. Nobody knew who the royalty was. They couldn't even suspect.

Big? Sure, they were big. But then even the big ones would hear the word and their bigness would start to leak out all the holes. I was thinking about it and wondering if they had heard it yet when Mousie Basso came in.

Guys like Mousie you see around when there's not too much light and never see around when the heat's on. Guys like Mousie you see in the papers when the police pull in their dragnet at a time when there were no holes in the walls for them to duck into. In the faces of guys like Mousie you can tell the temperature of the underworld caldron or read your popularity with the wrong people by the way they shy away or hang on to you.

From Mousie's face I knew I was hot.

I knew, too, I wasn't very popular.

Mousie took one look at me sitting there, shot a quick look at the door and would have been out if I hadn't been reaching inside my coat for a smoke at the time. Mousie got white past the point of being pale when he saw where my hand was and when I gave him the nod to come over, he didn't walk, he slunk.

I said, "Hello, Mousie," and the corner of his mouth made a fast, fake smile and he slid into the booth hoping nobody had seen him.

He grabbed a nervous cigarette that didn't do him a bit of good, shook out the match and flicked it under the table. "Look, Mr. Hammer, you and me ain't got a thing to talk about. I . . ."

"Maybe I like your company, Mousie."

His lips got tight and he tried hard to keep from watching my hands. Half under his breath he said, "You ain't good company to be seen with."

"Who says?"

"Lots of people. You're nuts, Mr. Hammer . . ." He waited to see what would happen and when nothing did, said, "you go blowing off your stack like you been doing and you'll be wearing a D.O.A. tag on your toe."

"I thought we were friends, kid." I bit into my sandwich and watched him squirm. Mousie wasn't happy. Not even a little bit.

"Okay, so you did me a favor. That doesn't make

us that kind of buddies. If you want trouble you go find it by yourself. Me, I'm a peace-loving guy, I am."

"Yeah."

Mousie's face sagged under the sarcasm. "So I'm a chiseler. So what? I don't want shooting trouble. If I'm small potatoes that's all I want to be. Nobody gets bumped for being small potatoes."

"Unless somebody sees them talking to big potatoes," I grinned at him.

It scared him, right down to his shoes. "Don't . . . don't kid around with me, will you? You don't need me for nothing. Besides which if you do I ain't giving or selling. Lay off."

"What did you hear, Mousie?"

His eyes were quick things that swept the whole room twice before they came back to me. "You know."

"What?"

"You're going to scramble some people."

"What people." I didn't ask him. I told him to say it.

He whispered the word. "Mafia." Then as if it had been a key he swallowed he spilled over with the things he had been holding down while his eyes bulged in his head. His hands grabbed the edge of the table and hung on while the butt he had started to smoke burned through the tablecloth. "You're nuts. You went and got everybody hopped up. Wherever you go you'll be poison. Is it true you got something on the wheels? You better clam if you have. That kind of stuff

is sure to lead to trouble. Charlie Max and Sugar
. . ." The mouth stopped and stayed open.

"Say it, Mousie."

Maybe he didn't like the way I had edged forward. Maybe he saw the things that should have
been written across my face.

The bulging eyes flattened out, sick. "They're
spending advance money along the Stem."

"Moving fast?"

I could hardly hear his voice. "Covering the bars
and making phone calls."

"Are they in a hurry?"

"Bonus, probably."

Mousie wasn't the same guy who came in. He
was the mouse, but a mouse who didn't care any
more. He was the mouse who spilled his guts to
the cat about where the dog was and if the dog
found out, he was dead. He reached for the remains
of the cigarette, tried to drag some life into it and
couldn't make it. I shook a new one out of my
pack and handed it to him. The light I held out
was steady, but he couldn't keep the tip of the
butt in it. He got it going after a few seconds and
stared into the flame of the lighter.

"You ain't scared a bit, are you?" He looked
at his own hands, hating himself. "I wish I was
that way. What makes a guy like me, Mr. Hammer?"

I could hate myself too. "Guys like me," I said.

The laugh came out his nose like he didn't believe me. "One guy," he said, "just one big guy
and everybody gets hopped up. For anybody else,

even the mayor, they wouldn't even blink, but for you they get hopped up. You say you're going to scramble and they make like a hillbilly feud. The word goes out and money starts passing hands. Two of the hottest rods in town combing the joints looking for you and you don't even get bothered enough to stop eating. They know you, Mr. Hammer. Guess maybe everybody knows something about you. That's why Charlie Max and Sugar Smallhouse got the job. They don't know nothing about you. They're Miami boys. You say you're going to do something, you do it and always there's somebody dead and it ain't you. Now the word has it you're going to scramble the top potatoes. Maybe you will and maybe you won't. With anybody else I'd take bets on your side, only this time it's different."

He stopped and waited to see what I'd say. "It's not so different."

"You'll find out."

He saw my teeth through the smile and shuddered. It does funny things to some people. "The world still goes," I said. "From now on to the end they'll have to stay away from windows and doors. They'll never be able to go out alone. Every one of the pack will have to keep a rod in his fist and wait. They'll have to double check everything to make sure I won't find out who they are and no matter how hard they try I'll reach them. Their office boys'll try to check me off but they're like flies on the wall. I'm going to the top. Straight up. I'm finding out who they are and when I do

106

they're dead. I know how they operate . . . they're bad, but they know me and I'm worse. No matter where I find them, or when . . . any time, any place . . . that's it. The top dogs, those are the ones I want. The slime who pull the strings in the Mafia. The kings, you understand? I want them."

My grin got bigger all the time. "They've killed hundreds of people, see, but they finally killed the wrong dame. They tried to kill me and they wrecked my car. That last part I especially didn't like. That car was hand built and could do over a hundred. And for all of that a lot of those top dogs are paying through the kiester starting now. That's the word."

Mousie didn't say anything. He stood up slowly, his teeth holding his bottom lip to keep it up. He jerked his head in what was supposed to be a so-long and slid out from behind the table. I watched him walk to the door, forgetting the sandwich that lay on top of the counter. He opened the door slowly, walked out to the sidewalk and turned east, not looking to either side of himself. When he had gone I got up myself, paid my bill and took the change to a phone booth.

Pat was home and still up. I said, "It's me, pal. Velda told me you heard the news."

He sounded a little far away. "You don't have much sense, do you?"

"They're looking for me. Two boys by the name of Charlie Max and Sugar Smallhouse."

"They have reps."

"So I hear. What kind?"

"Teamwork. Max is the one to watch. They're killers, but Smallhouse likes to do it slow."

"I'll watch Max then. What else?"

"Charlie Max is an ex-cop. He'll probably have a preference for a hip holster."

"Thanks."

"Don't mention it."

I slapped the receiver back on the hook. The dime plinked into the box and the gaping mouth of the thing laughed at me silently. Well, in a way it was a pretty big joke. The army of silent men couldn't stay silent. I didn't know them but they knew me. They were just like the rest; crumbs who knew how to play a one-sided game, but when they were playing somebody who could be twice as silent, twice as dirty and twice as quick they broke in the middle and started begging. Someplace in the city were people with names and some without names. They were organized. They had big money in back of them. They had political connections. They had everything it took to stay where they were except one thing and that was me with my own slab in a morgue. They know what to expect from the cops and what to expect from the vast machine that squatted on the Potomac but they didn't know what to expect from me. Already one guy had told them, a punk with crooked yellow teeth who had had a gun on me and lost it. Then they'd ask around if they didn't already know and the stories they'd hear wouldn't be pretty. The fear they handed out so freely to others they'd taste themselves, knowing that before long, if I was still alive, they'd have to chew the whole lump and swallow it.

At the cigarette counter I picked up a fresh deck of Luckies, went out into the air and headed for the Stem. Out there were the hunters spending advance money. Cold boys with reps who didn't know the whole score. They knew the word was out and wanted to cut it off.

But they didn't hear the whole word. Before the night was over they'd hear a lot of things that might make them want to change their minds. One of the things was the rest of the word. They'd find out the hunters were being hunted.

Just for the fun of it.

Chapter Eight

The *Globe* gave me the information on Nicholas Raymond. It was an old clipping that Ray Diker dragged out for me and which wouldn't have been printed at all if there hadn't been an editorial tie-up. The press was hot on hit-and-run drivers and used his case to point up their arguments about certain light conditions along the bridge approaches.

Nicholas Raymond got it as he stepped into the street as the light changed and his body was flung through a store window. Nobody saw the accident except a drunk halfway down the block and the car was never tracked down. The only details about him were that he was forty-two years old, a small-time importer and lived in an apartment hotel in the lower Fifties.

I told Ray Diker thanks and used his phone to call Raymond's old address. The manager told me in a thick accent that yes, he remembered Mr. Nick-o-las Raymondo, he was the fine man who always paid his bills and tipped like a gentleman extreme. It was too bad he should die. I agreed with him, poked around for some personal information and found that he was the kind nothing can be said about. Apparently he was clean.

Finding something on McGrath was easy. The papers carried the same stuff Velda had passed to me without adding anything to it. Ray made a couple calls downstairs and supplied the rest. Walter McGrath was a pretty frequent visitor to some of the gaudier night clubs around town and generally had a pretty chick in tow. A little persuasion and Ray managed to get his address. A big hotel on Madison Avenue. The guy was really living.

We sat there a few minutes and Ray asked, "Anything else?"

"Lee Kawolsky. Remember him?"

Ray didn't have to go to his files for that. "Good boy, Mike. It was a shame he couldn't follow through. Broke his hand in training and it never healed properly. He could have been a champ."

"What did he do for a living after that?"

"Let's see." Ray's face wrinkled in thought. "Seems like he bartended for Ed Rooney a bit, then he was doing a little training work with some of the other fighters. Wait a sec." He picked up the phone again, called Sports and listened for a minute to the droning voice on the other end. When he hung up he had a question in his eyes.

"What's the pitch, Mike?"

"Like what?"

His eyes sharpened a bit as they watched me. "Lee went to work for a private detective agency that specialized in supplying bodyguards for society brawls and stuff. One of his first assignments

111

was sticking with a kid who was killed across the river a few days ago."

"Interesting," I said.

"Very. How about the story angle?"

"If I knew that I wouldn't be here now. How did he die?"

"It wasn't murder."

"Who says?"

He picked up a pipe, cradled it in his hand and began to scrape the bowl with a penknife. "Killers don't drive the same beer truck for ten years. They aren't married with five kids and don't break down and cry on the street when they've had their first accident."

"You got a good memory, kid."

"I was at the funeral, Mike. I was interested enough to find out what happened."

"Any witnesses?"

"Not a one."

I stood up and slapped my hat on. "Thanks for the stuff, Ray. If I get anything I'll let you know."

"Need any help?"

"Plenty. There's three names you can work on. Dig up anything good and I'll make it worth your while."

"All I want is an exclusive."

"Maybe you'll get one."

He grinned at me and stuck the pipe in his mouth. Ray wasn't much of a guy. He was little and skinny and tight as hell with a buck, but he could get places fast when he wanted to. I grinned back, waved and took the elevator to the street.

Dr. Martin Soberin had his office facing Central Park. It wasn't the world's best location, but it came close. It took in a corner, was blocked in white masonry with Venetian shuttered windows and a very discreet sign that announced his residency. The sign said he was in so I pushed open the door while the chimes inside toned my arrival.

Inside it was better than I thought it would be. There was a neat, precise air about the place that said here was a prominent medical man suited to the needs of the upper crust, yet certainly within the financial and confidential range of absolutely anybody. Books lined the walls, professional journals were neatly stacked on the table and the furniture had been chosen and arranged to put any patient at ease. I sat down, started to light a cigarette and stopped in the middle of it when the nurse walked in.

Some women are just pretty. Some are just beautiful. Some are just gorgeous. Some are like her. For a minute you think somebody slammed one to your belly then your breath comes back with a rush and you hope she doesn't move out of the light that makes a translucent screen out of the white nylon uniform.

But she does and she says hello and you feel all gone all over.

She's got light chestnut hair and her voice is just right. She's got eyes to go with the hair and they sweep over you and laugh because she knows how you feel. And only for a moment do the eyes show disappointment because somehow the cigarette gets lit as if she hadn't been there at all and the smoke from my mouth smooths out any expression I might have let show through.

"The doctor in?"

"Yes, but he's with a patient right now. He'll be finished shortly."

"I'll wait," I said.

"Would you care to step inside while I make out a card for you?"

I took a pull on the Lucky and let it out in a fast, steady stream. I stood up so I could look down at her, grinning a little bit. "Right now that would be the nicest thing I could think of, but I'm not exactly a patient."

She didn't change her expression. Her eyebrows went up slightly and she said, "Oh?"

"Let's say I'll pay the regular rates if it's necessary."

The eyebrows came down again. "I don't think that will be necessary." Her smile was a quick, friendly one. "Is there any way I can help you?"

I grinned bigger and the smile changed to a short laugh.

"Please," she said.

"How long will the doctor be?"

"Another half hour perhaps."

"Okay, then maybe you can do it. I'm an investigator. The name is Michael Hammer, if it means anything to you. Right now I'd like to get some information on a girl named Berga Torn. A short while back Dr. Soberin okayed her for a rest cure at a sanitarium."

"Yes. Yes, I remember her. Perhaps you'd better come inside after all."

Her smile was a challenge no man could put up with. She opened the door, walked into the light again and over to a desk in the corner. She turned around, saw me standing there in the doorway and smoothed out her skirt with a motion of her hands. I could hear the static jump all the way across the room and the fabric clung even closer than it had.

"You'd be surprised how fast a person decides he really isn't sick after all," she said.

"What about the women patients?"

"They get sicker." Her mouth pursed in a repressed laugh. "What are you thinking?"

I walked over to the desk and pulled up the straight-backed chair. "Why a dish like you takes a job like this."

"If you must know, fame and fortune." She pulled out a file case and began to thumb through the cards.

"Try it again," I said.

She looked up quickly. "Truly interested?"

I nodded.

"I studied to be a nurse right after high school. I graduated, and quite unfortunately, won a beauty contest before I could start practicing. A week later I was in Hollywood sitting on my . . . sitting around posing for stills and nothing more. Six months later I was car-hopping at a drive-in diner and it took me another year to get wise. So I came home and became a nurse."

"So you were a lousy actress?"

She smiled and shook her head.

"It couldn't have been that you didn't have a figure after all?"

Her cheeks sucked in poutingly and her eyes looked up at me with a you-should-know-better expression. "Funny enough," she said, "I wasn't photogenic. Imagine that?"

"No, I can't."

She sat up with three typewritten cards in her hand. "Thank you, Mr. Hammer." Her voice was a song of some hidden forest bird that made you stop whatever you were doing to listen. She laid the cards out in front of her, the smile fading away. "I believe this is what you came for. Now can I see your insurance credentials, and if you have your forms I'll . . ."

"I'm not an insurance investigator."

She gave me a quizzical look and automatically gathered the cards together. "Oh . . . I'm sorry. You know, of course, that this information is always confidential and . . ."

"The girl is dead. She was murdered."

She went to say something and stopped short. Then: "Police?"

I nodded and hoped she didn't say anything more.

"I see." Her teeth pinched her lower lip and she looked sideways at the door to her left. "If I remember I believe the doctor had another policeman in to see him not long ago."

"That's right. I'm following up on the case. I'd

like to go over everything personally instead of from reports. If you'd rather wait for the doctor . . ."

"Oh, no, I think it will be all right. Shall I read these off to you?"

"Shoot."

"To be brief, she was in an extremely nervous condition. Overwork, apparently. She was hysterical here in the office and the doctor had to administer a sedative. Complete rest was the answer and the doctor arranged for her to be admitted to the sanitarium." Her eyebrows pulled together slightly. "Frankly, I can't possibly see what there is here to interest the police. There was no physical disorder except symptoms brought on by her mental condition."

"Could I see the cards?"

"Certainly." She handed them to me and leaned forward on the desk, thought better of it when my head turned, smiled and sat back again.

I didn't bother with the card she had read from. The first gave the patient's name, address, previous medical history and down at the bottom along the left side was the notation RECOMMENDED BY and next to it was the name William Wieton. The other card gave the diagnosis, suggested treatment and corroboration from the sanitarium that the diagnosis was correct.

I looked at the cards again, made a face at the complete lack of information they gave me, then handed them back.

"They help any?"

"Oh, you can never tell."

"Would you still like to see the doctor?"

"Not specially. Maybe I'll be back."

Something happened to her face. "Please do."

She didn't get up this time. I walked to the door, looked back and she was sitting there with her chin in her hands watching me. "You ought to give Hollywood another try," I said.

"I meet more interesting people here," she told me. Then added, "Though it's hard to tell on such short acquaintance."

I winked, she winked back and I went out on the street.

Broadway had bloomed again. It was there in all its colorful glory, stretching wide-open arms to the sucker, crying out with a voice that was never still. I walked toward the lights trying to think, trying to put bits together and add pieces where the holes were.

I found a delicatessen, went in and had a sandwich. I came out and headed up Broadway, making the stops as I came to them. Two hours went by in a hurry and nothing had happened. No, I didn't stay on the Stem because nobody would be looking for me on the Stem. Later maybe, but not now.

So I got off the Stem and went east where the people talked different and dressed different and were my kind of people. They didn't have dough and they didn't have flash, but behind their eyes was the knowledge of the city and the way it thought and ran. They were people who were afraid of the monster that grew up around them and showed it, yet they couldn't help liking it.

I made my stops and worked my way down to the Twenties.

I had caught the looks, seen the nods and heard the whispers.

At any time now I could have picked the boys out of a line-up by sight from the descriptions that came to me in an undertone.

In one place something else was added. There were others to watch for too.

Two-thirty and I had missed them by ten minutes.

The next half hour and they seemed to have lost themselves.

I got back to the Stem before all of the joints started closing down. The cabbie dropped me on a corner and I started the rounds on foot. In two places they were glad to see me and in the third the bartender who had pushed a lot of them my way tried to shut the door in my face, mumbling excuses that he was through for the night. I wedged it open, shoved him back inside and leaned against it until it clicked shut.

"The boys were here, Andy?"

"Mike, I don't like this."

"I don't either. When?"

"About an hour ago."

"You know them?"

His head bobbed and he glanced past me out the side window. "They were pointed out to me."

"Sober?"

"Two drinks. They barely touched 'em." I waited while he looked past me again. "The little guy was nervous. Edgy. He wanted a drink but the other one squashed it."

Andy ran his hands down under his fat waistband to keep them still. "Mike . . . nobody's to say a word to you. This is rough stuff. Do you . . . well, sort of stay clear of here until things blow over."

"Nothing's blowing over, friend. I want you to pass it around where it'll get heard. Tell the boys to stay put. I'll find them. They don't have to go looking for me any more."

"Jeepers, Mike."

"Tell it where it'll get heard."

My fingers found the door and pulled it open. The street outside was empty and a cop was standing on the corner. A squad car went by and he saluted it. Two drunks turned the corner behind his back and mimicked him with thumbs to their noses.

I turned my key in the lock. I knew the chain should be on so I opened the door a couple of inches and said, "It's me, Lily."

There was no sound at first, then only that of a deeply drawn breath being let out slowly. The light from the corner lamp was on, giving the room an empty appearance. She drifted into it silently and the glow from her hair seemed to brighten it a little.

Something was tight and strange in the smile

she gave me through the opening in the door. Strange, faraway, curious. Something I couldn't put my finger on. It was there, then it was gone and she had the door unhooked and I stepped inside.

It was my turn to haul in my breath. She stood there almost breathlessly, looking up at me. Her mouth was partly open and I could see her tongue working behind her teeth. For some reason her eyes seemed to float there, two separate dark wells that could knead your flesh until it crawled.

Then she smiled, and the light that gilded her hair made shadows across the flat of her stomach and I could see the lush contours harden with an eager anticipation that was like her first expression . . . there, then suddenly gone like a frightened bird.

I said, "You didn't have to wait up."

"I . . . couldn't sleep."

"Anybody call?"

"Two. I didn't answer." Her fingers felt for the buttons on the robe, satisfied themselves that they were all there from her chin down to her knees, an unconscious gesture that must have been a habit. "Someone was here." The thought of it widened her eyes.

"Who?"

"They knocked. They tried the door." Her voice was almost a whisper. I could see the tremor in her chin and from someplace in the past I could feel the hate pounding into my head and my fingers wanted to squeeze something bad.

Her eyes drifted away from mine slowly. "How scared can a person get, Mike?" she asked. "How . . . scared?"

I reached out for her, took her face in my hands and tilted it up. Her eyes were warm and misty and her mouth a hungry animal that wanted to bite or be bitten, a questioning thing waiting to be tasted and I wanted to tell her she never had to be scared again. Not ever.

But I couldn't because my own mouth was too close and she pulled away with a short, frenzied jerk that had a touch of horror in it and she was out of reach.

It didn't last long. She smiled and I remembered her telling me I was a nice guy and nice guys have to be careful even when the lady has been around. Especially a lady who has just stepped out of the tub to open the door for you and had nothing to put on but a very sheer silk robe and you know what happens when those things get wet. The smile deepened and sparkled at me, then she drifted to the bedroom and the door closed.

I heard her moving around in there, heard her get into the bed, then I sat down in the chair facing the window and turned out the light. I switched the radio on to a late station, sitting there, seeing nothing at all, my mind miles away up in the mountains. I was coming around a curve and then there was that Viking girl standing there waving at me. She was in the beams of the lights, the tires shrieking to a stop, and she got closer and closer until there was no hope of stopping the car at all. She let out one final scream that had all the terror in the world in it and I could feel the sweat running down the back of my neck. Even when she was dead under the wheels the screaming didn't stop, then my eyes came open and my ears heard again and I picked up the phone and her cry stopped entirely.

I said a short hello into it, said it again and then a voice, a nice gentle voice asked me if this was Mike Hammer.

"That's right," I said. "Who's this?"

"It really doesn't matter, Mr. Hammer. I merely wanted to call your attention to the fact that as you go out today please notice the new car in front of your building. It belongs to you. The papers are on the seat and all you have to do is sign them and transfer your plates."

It was a long foul smell that seeped right through the receiver. "What's the rest of it, friend?"

The voice, the nice gentle voice, stopped purring and took on an insidious growl. "The rest of it is that we're sorry about your other car. Very sorry. It was too bad, but since things happened as they did, other things must change."

"Finish it."

"You can have the car, Mr. Hammer. I suggest that if you take it you use it to go on a long vacation. Say about three or four months?"

"If I don't?"

"Then leave it where it is. We'll see that it is returned to the buyer."

I laughed into the phone. I made it a mean,

low kind of laugh that didn't need any words to go with it. I said, "Buddy . . . I'll take the car, but I won't take the vacation. Someday I'll take you too."

"However you wish."

I said, "That's the way it always is," but I was talking to a dead phone. The guy had hung up.

They were at me from both ends now. The boys walking around the Stem on a commission basis. One eye out for me, the other for the cops that Pat would have scouting. Now they were being generous.

Like Lily had said, how scared could a person get? They didn't like the way it was going at all. I sat there grinning at the darkness outside thinking about the big boys whose faces nobody knew. Maybe if I had boiled over like the old days they would have had me. The waiting they didn't go for.

I shook a Lucky out of the pack and lit it up. I smoked it down to the end, put it out, then went in and flopped down on the bed. The alarm was set for eight, too early even at that hour, but I set it back to seven and knew I'd be hating myself for it.

The heap was a beauty. It was a maroon Ford convertible with a black top and sat there gleaming in the early morning sunlight like a dew drop. Bob Gellie walked around it once, grinning into the chrome and came back and stood by me on the sidewalk.

"Some job, Mike. Got twin pipes in back." He wiped his hands on his cover-alls and waited to see what came next.

"She's gimmicked, Bob. Think you can reach it?"

"Come again?" He stared at me curiously.

"The job is a gift . . . from somebody who doesn't like me. They're hoping I step into it. Then goes the big boom. They're probably even smart enough to figure I'd put a mechanic on the job to find the gimmick so it'll be well hidden. Go ahead and dig it out."

He wiped the back of his hands across his mouth and shoved the hat back further on his head. "Best thing to do is run it in the river for a couple of hours."

"Hop to it, Bob, I need transportation."

"Look, for a hundred I can do a lot of things, but . . ."

"So I'll double it. Find the gimmick."

The two C's got him. For that many pieces of paper he could take his chances with a gallon of soup. He wiped his mouth clean again and nodded. The sun wasn't up over the apartments yet and it was still cool, but it didn't do much for the beads of sweat that started to shape up along Bob's forehead. I went down to a restaurant, filled up with breakfast, spent an hour looking in store windows and came back.

Bob was sitting behind the wheel looking thoughtful, the hood in front of him raised up like a kid with his thumb to his nose. He got out when he saw me, lit a cigarette and pointed to the engine. "She's hot, Mike. A real conversion."

I could see what he meant. The heads were finned aluminum jobs flanking dual carburetors and the headers that came off the manifold poked back in a graceful sweep.

"Wonder what she's like inside?"

"Probably complete. Think your old heap could take this baby?"

"I haven't even driven this one yet. Find the stuff?"

His mouth tightened and he looked around him once, fast. "Yeah. Six sticks wired to the ignition."

"It stinks."

"That's what I thought too," he told me. "Couldn't find a thing anyplace else though. Checked the whole assembly inside and out and if there's more of it the guy who placed it sure knew his business."

"He does, Bob. He's an expert at it."

I stood there while he finished his butt. He walked around the hood, got down under the car and poked around there, then came back and looked at the engine again.

Then his face changed, went back a half dozen years into the past, got tight, relaxed into a puzzled grin, then he looked at me and snorted. "Bet I got it, Mike."

"How much?"

"Another hundred?"

"You're on."

"I remember a booby trap they set on a Heinie

general's car once. A real cutie." He grinned again. "Missed the general but got his driver a couple of days later."

He slid into the car, bent down under the dash and worked at something with his screwdriver. He got out looking satisfied, shoved his tools under the car and crawled in with them. The job took another twenty minutes and when he came out he was moving slowly, balancing something in his hand. It looked like a section of pipe cut lengthwise and from one end protruded a detonation cap.

"There she is," he said. "Nice, huh?"

"Yeah."

"Rigged to the speedometer. A few hundred miles from now a contact would have been made and you'd be dust. Had the thing wrapped around the top section of the muffler. What'll I do with it?"

"Drop it in the river, Bob. Keep the deal to yourself. Drop up to my place tonight and I'll write you a check."

He looked at the thing in his hand, shuddered and held it even tighter. "Er . . . if it doesn't mean anything to you, Mike . . . I'd like to have the dough now."

"I'm good for it. What're you worried . . ."

"I know, I know, but if anybody's after you this bad you might not live to tonight. Understand?"

I understood. I went up and wrote him out a check, gave him an extra buck for the cab fare to the river and got in the car. It wasn't a bad buy at all for three C's. And one buck. Then I started it up, felt good when I heard the low, throaty growl that poured out of the twin pipes and eased the shift into gear for the short haul north.

Pat had been wrong about Carl Evello being in the city. In one week he had gone through two addresses and the last was the best. Carl Evello lived in Yonkers, a very exclusive section of Yonkers.

At first the place seemed modest, then you noticed the meticulous care somebody gave the garden, and saw the Cadillac convertible and new Buick sedan that made love together in a garage that would have looked well as a wing on the Taj Mahal. The house must have gone to twenty rooms at the least and nothing was left out.

I rolled up the hard-topped driveway and stopped. From someplace behind the house I could hear the pleasant laughter of women and the faint strains of a radio. A man laughed and another joined him.

I cut the engine and climbed out, trying to decide whether I should crash the party or go through the regular channels. I started around the car when I heard tires turn into the driveway and while I stood there a light-green Merc drove up behind me, honked a short note of hello, revved up fast and stopped.

Beauty is a funny thing. Like all babies are beautiful no matter how they're shaped. Like how there are times when any woman is beautiful as long as she's the color you want. It's not something that only shows in a picture. It's a composite something that you can't quite describe, but can recognize the second you see it and that's the way this woman was.

Her hair was a pale brown ocean that swirled with motion and threw off the sunlight that bounced into it. She smiled at me, her mouth a gorgeous curve that had a peculiar attraction so that you almost missed the body that bore it. Her mouth was full and wet as if it had just been licked, a lush mouth with a will of its own and always hungry.

She walked up with a long stride, pressing against the breeze, smiling a little. And when she smiled her mouth twisted a bit in the corner with an even hungrier look and she said, "Hi. Going to the social?"

"I wasn't," I said. "Business, now I'm sorry."

Her teeth came out from under the soft curves and the laugh filled her throat. For the barest second she gave me a critical glance, frowned with a mixture of perplexed curiosity and the smile got a shade bigger. "You're a little different, anyway," she said.

I didn't answer and she stuck out her hand. "Michael Friday."

I grinned back and took it. "Mike Hammer."

"Two Mikes."

"Looks like it. You'll have to change your name."

"Uh-uh. You do it."

"You were right the first time . . . I'm different. I tell, not get told."

Her hand squeezed in mine and the laugh blotted out all the sounds that were around us. "Then I'll stay Michael . . . for a time, anyway." I dropped her hand and she said, "Looking for Carl?"

"That's right."

"Well, whatever your business is, maybe I can help you out. The butler will tell you he isn't in so let's not ask him, okay?"

"Okay," I said.

This, I thought, is the way they should be. Friendly and uncomplicated. Let the good breeding show. Let it stick out all over for anybody to see. That was beauty. The kind that took your hand as if you were lovers and had known each other a lifetime, picking up a conversation as if you had merely been interrupted in one already started.

We took the flagstone path that led around the house through the beds of flowers, not hurrying a bit, but taking in the fresh loveliness of the place.

I handed her a cigarette, lit it, then did mine.

As she let the smoke filter through her lips she said, "What *is* your business, by the way? Do I introduce you as a friend or what?"

Her mouth was too close and too hungry looking. It wasn't trying to be that way. It just was, like a steak being grilled over an open fire when you're starved. I took a drag on my own butt and found her eyes. "I don't sell anything, Michael . . . not unless it's trouble. I could be wrong, but I doubt if I'll need much of an introduction to Carl."

"I don't understand."

"Sometime look up my history. Any paper will supply the dope."

I got looked at then like a prize specimen in a cage. "I think I will, Mike," she smiled, "but I don't think anything I find will surprise me." The smile went into that deep laugh again as we turned the corner of the building.

And there was Carl Evello.

He wasn't anything special. You could pass him on the street and figure him for a businessman, but nothing more. He was in his late forties, an average-looking joe starting to come out at the middle a bit but careful enough to dress right so it didn't show. He mixed drinks at a table shaded by a beach umbrella, laughing at the three girls who relaxed in steamer chairs around him.

The two men with him could have been other businessmen if you didn't know that one pulled the strings in a racket along the waterfront that made him a front-page item every few months.

The other one didn't peddle forced labor, hot merchandise or tailor-made misery, but his racket was just as dirty. He had an office in Washington somewhere and peddled influence. He shook hands with presidents and ex-cons alike and got rich on the proceeds of his introductions.

I would have felt better if the conversation had stopped when I walked over. Then I would have known. But nothing stopped. The girls smiled pleasantly and said hello. Carl studied me during the name swapping, his expression one of trying to recall an image of something that should have been familiar.

Then he said, "Hammer, Mike Hammer. Well, of course. Private detective, aren't you?"

"I was."

"Certainly. I've read about you quite often. Leave it to my sister to find someone unusual for an escort." He smiled broadly, his whole face beaming with pleasure. "I'd like you to meet Al Affia, Mr. Hammer. Mr. Affia is a business representative of a Brooklyn outfit."

The boy from the waterfront pulled his face into a crooked smile and stuck out his hand. I felt like whacking him in the mouth.

I said, "Hello," instead and laughed into his eyes like he was laughing in mine because we had met a long time ago and both knew it.

Leo Harmody didn't seem to do anything. His hand was sticky with sweat and a little too limp. He repeated my name once, nodded and went back to his girl.

Carl said, "Drink?"

"No thanks. If you got a few minutes I'd like to speak to you."

"Sure, sure."

"This isn't a social visit."

"Hell, hardly anybody comes to see me socially. Don't feel out of place. This a private talk?"

"Yeah."

"Let's go inside." He didn't bother to excuse himself. He picked up a fresh drink, nodded to me and started across the lawn toward the house. The two goons sitting on the steps got up respectfully, held the door open and followed us in.

The house was just what I expected it to be. A million bucks properly framed and hung. A fortune in good taste that didn't come from the mouth of a guy who started life on the outer fringe of a mob. We went through a long hall, stepped into a study dominated by a grand piano at one end and Carl waved me to a chair.

The two goons closed the door and stood with their backs to it. I said, "This is a private talk."

Carl waved unconcernedly. "They don't hear anything," then sipped his drink. Only his eyes showed over the lip of the glass. They were almond shaped and beady. They were the kind of eyes I had seen too many times before, hard little diamonds nestling in their soft cushions of fat.

I looked at the goons and one grinned, rising on his toes and rocking back and forth. Both of them had a bulge on the right hip that meant just one thing. They were loaded. "They still have ears."

"They still don't hear anything. Only what I want them to hear." His face beamed into a smile. "They're necessary luxuries, you might say. There seem to be people who constantly make demands on me, if you know what I mean."

"I know what you mean." I pulled a cigarette out and tapped thoughtfully against the arm of the chair. Then I let him watch me make a smile, turning a little so the two goons could see it too.

"But they're not worth a damn, Carl, not a damn. I could kill you and the both of them before any one of you could get a rod in his fist."

Carl half rose and the big goon stopped rocking. For a second he stood that way and it looked like he'd try it. I let my smile tighten up at the edges and he didn't try it after all. Carl said, "Outside, boys."

They went outside.

"Now we can talk," I said.

"I don't like that kind of stuff, Mr. Hammer."

"Yeah. It spoils 'em. They know they're not the hot rods they're paid off for being. It's kind of funny when you think of it. Put a guy real close to dying and he changes. I mean real close. They're only tough because they're different from ordinary people. They have little consciences and nothing bothers them. They can shoot a guy and laugh because they know they probably won't get shot back at, but like I said, let 'em get real close to dying and they change. They found out something right away. I got a little conscience too."

All the time I was speaking he was half out of his chair. Now he slid back into it again and picked up his drink. "Your business, Mr. Hammer."

"A girl. Her name was Berga Torn."

His nostrils seemed to flare out a little. "I understand she died."

"Was killed."

"And your interest in it?"

"Let's not waste time, you and me," I said.

"You can talk to me now or I can do it the hard way. Take your pick."

"Listen, Mr. Hammer . . ."

"Shut up. You listen. I want to hear you tell me about your connection with the dame. Nothing else. No crap. You play games with somebody else, but not me. I'm not the law, but plenty of times there were guys who wished the law was around instead of me."

It was hard to tell what he was thinking. His eyes seemed to harden, then melted into the smile that creased his mouth. "All right, Mr. Hammer, there's no need to get nasty about anything. I've told the police exactly what the score was and it isn't important enough to keep back from you if you're genuinely interested. Berga Torn was a girl I liked. For a while back there I . . . well, kept her, you might say."

"Why?"

"Don't be ridiculous. If you knew her then you know why."

"She didn't have much to offer that you couldn't get someplace else."

"She had enough. Now, what else is there?"

"Why did you break it off?"

"Because I felt like it. She was getting in my hair. I thought you had a reputation with women. You should know what it's like."

"I didn't know you checked up on me that close, Carl."

The eyes went hard again. "I thought we weren't playing games now."

135

I lit the cigarette I was fooling with, taking my time with that first drag. "How do you stand with the Mafia, Carl?"

He played it nice. Nothing showed at all, not even a little bit. "That's going pretty far."

"Yeah, I guess it is." I stuck the cigarette in my mouth and stood up. "But it's not nearly as far as it's going to go." I started for the door.

His glass hit the desk top and he came forward in his seat again. "You sure put up a big stink for a lot of small talk, Mr. Hammer."

I turned around and smiled at him, a nice dead kind of smile that had no laugh behind it and I could see him go tight from where I stood. I said, "I wasn't after talk, Carl. I wanted to see your face. I wanted to know it so I'd never forget it. Someday I'm going to watch it turn blue or maybe bleed to death. Your eyes'll get all wide and sticky and your tongue will hang out and I won't be making any mistake about it being the wrong joe. Think about it Carl, especially when you go to bed at night."

I turned the knob and opened the door.

The two boys were standing there. All they did was look at me and it wasn't with much affection. I was going to have to remember them too.

When I got back outside Michael Friday spotted me and waved. I didn't wave back so she came over, a mock frown across her face. I couldn't get my eyes off her mouth, even when she faked a pout. "Bum steer," she said, "no business?"

She looked like a kid, a very beautiful kid and

all grown up where it counted, but with the grin and impishness of a kid nevertheless. And you don't get sore at kids. "I hear you're his sister."

"Not quite. We had the same mother but came from different hatches."

"Oh."

"Going to join the party?"

I looked over at the group still downing the drinks. "No thanks. I don't like the company."

"Neither do I for that matter. Let's both leave."

"Now you got something," I said.

We didn't even bother with good-byes. She just grabbed my arm and steered me around the building talking a blue streak about nothing at all. We made the front as a car was coming up the driveway and as I was opening the door of my new heap it stopped and a guy got out in a hurry, trotted around the side and opened the door.

I started wondering what the eminent Congressman Geyfey was doing up this way when he was supposed to be serving on a committee in Washington. Then I stopped wondering when he took the woman's arm and helped her out and Velda smiled politely in our direction a moment before going up the path.

Michael said, "Stunning, isn't she?"

"Very. Who is she?"

She stayed deadpan because she meant it. Her head moved slightly as she said, "I don't know. Most likely one of Bob's protégés. He seems to do very well for himself."

"He doesn't if he overlooked you."

Her laugh was quick and fresh. "Thank you, but he didn't overlook me, I overlooked him."

"Nice for me," I grinned. "What's a congressman doing with Carl? He may be your brother, but his reputation's got spots on it."

Her grin didn't fade a bit. "My brother certainly isn't the most ethical man I've known, but he is big business, and in case you haven't known about it, big business and government go hand in hand sometimes."

"Uh-uh. Not Carl's kind of business."

This time her frown wasn't put on. She studied me while she slid into the car and waited until I was behind the wheel. "Before Bob was elected he was Carl's lawyer. He handled some corporation account Carl had out West." She stopped and looked into my eyes. "It's wrong someplace, isn't it?"

"Frankly, Friday gal, it stinks."

I started the engine, sat and listened to it purr a minute then eased the gearshift in. All that power under the hood was dying to let go and I sat on it. I took the heap down the drive, rolled out to the street and swung toward the center of town. We didn't talk. We sat and rode for a while and watched the houses drift past. The sun was high overhead, a warm ball that smiled at the world, a big warm thing that made everything seem all right when everything was so damned wrong.

Pretty soon it would come. I thought about how she'd put it and how I'd answer it. It could come guarded, veiled or in a roundabout way, but it would come.

When it did come it was right out in the open and she asked, "What did you want with Carl?" Her voice sounded sleepy and relaxed. I glanced at her lying back there so lazily against the cushions, her hair spilling down the back of the seat. Her mouth was still a wet thing, deliciously red, firm, yet ready to vibrate like the strings on a fiddle the moment they were touched.

I answered her the same way she asked it; right out in the open. "He had a girl once. She's dead now and he may be involved in her murder. Your big-business brother may have a Mafia tie-up."

Her head rolled on the seat until she was looking at me. "And you?"

"When I get interested in people like your brother they usually wind up dead."

"Oh." That's all. Just "Oh" and she turned and looked out the window, staring straight ahead.

"You want me to take you back?"

"No."

"Want to talk about it?"

Her hand reached over and took the deck of Luckies from the seat beside me. She lit two at the same time and stuck one in my mouth. It tasted of lipstick, a nice taste. The kind that makes you want to taste it again, this time from the source.

"I'm surprised it took this long," she said. "He used to try to fool me, but now he doesn't bother. I've often wondered when it would happen." She breathed in deeply on the smoke, then watched it whip out the half-opened ventilator. "Do you mind if I cry a little bit?"

"Go ahead."

"Is it serious trouble?"

"You don't get more serious than killing somebody."

"But was it Carl?"

Her eyes were wet when they turned in my direction. "I don't know," I said.

"Then you're not sure?"

"That's right. But then again, I don't have to be sure."

"But . . . you're the police?"

"Nope. Not anybody. Just such an important nobody that a whole lot of people would like to see me knocked off. The only trouble is they can't make the grade."

I pulled the car to the curb, backed it into the slot in front of a gin mill and cut the engine. "You were talking about your brother."

She didn't look at me. She worked the cigarette down to a stub and flipped it into the gutter. "There isn't much to tell, really. I know what he's been and I know the people he's associated with. They aren't what you would call the best people, though he mixes with them too. Generally he has something they want."

"Ever hear of Berga Torn?"

"Yes, I remember her well. I thought Carl had quite a crush on her. He . . . kept her for a long time."

"Why did he dump her?"

"I . . . I don't know." There was a catch in her voice. "She was a peculiar sort of girl. All I remember is that they had an argument one night and Carl never bothered with her much after that. Somebody new came along."

"That all?"

Michael nodded.

"Ever hear of the Mafia?"

She nodded again. "Mike . . . Carl isn't . . . one of those people. I know he isn't."

"You wouldn't know about it if he was."

"And if he is?"

I shrugged. There was only one answer to a question like that.

Her fingers were a little unsteady when they picked up another cigarette. "Mike . . . I'd like to go back now."

I lit the butt for her and kicked the motor over. She sat there, smoked it out and had another. Never talking. Not seeming to do anything at all. Her bottom lip was puffed up from chewing on it and every few minutes her shoulders would twitch as she repressed a sob. I drove up to the gateway of the house, leaned across her and opened the door.

"Friday . . ."

"Yes, Mike?"

"If you think you know an answer to it . . . call me."

"All right, Mike." She started to get out, stopped and turned her head. "You looked like fun, Mike. For both of us, I'm honestly sorry."

Her mouth was too close and too soft to just look at. My fingers seemed to get caught in her hair and suddenly those lovely, wet lips were only inches away, and just as suddenly there was no distance at all.

The bubbling warmth was just what I expected. The fire and the cushiony softness and the vibrancy made a living bed of her mouth. I leaned into it, barely touched it and came away before there was too much hunger. The edges of her teeth showed in a faint smile and she touched my face with the tips of her fingers, then she climbed out of the car.

All the way back to Manhattan I could taste it. The warmth and the wetness and a tantalizing flavor.

The garage was filled so I parked at the curb, gassed up for an excuse to stay there and walked into the office. Bob Gellie was busy putting a distributor together, but he dropped it when I came in.

I said, "How did it go, kid?"

"Hi, Mike. You gave me a job, all right."

"Get it?"

"Yeah, I got it. I checked two dozen outlets before I found where those heads came from. A place out in Queens sold 'em. The rest of the stuff I couldn't get a line on at all. Most of it's done directly from California or Chicago."

"So?"

"They were ordered by phone and picked up and paid for by a messenger."

"Great."

"Want me to keep trying?"

"Never mind. Those boys have their own mechanics. What about the car?"

"Another cutie. It came out of the Bronx. The guy who bought it said it was a surprise for his partner. He paid cash. Like a jerk the dealer let him borrow his plates and it got driven down, the plates were taken off and handed back to the dealer again." He opened the drawer and slid an envelope across to me. "Here's your registration. I don't know how the hell they worked it but they did. Them guys left themselves wide open."

"Who bought the car?"

"Guess."

"Smith, Jones, Robinson. Who?"

"O'Brien. Clancy O'Brien. He was medium. Mr. Average Man. Nobody could describe him worth a hoot. You know the kind?"

"I know the kind. Okay, Bob, call it quits. It isn't worth pushing."

He nodded and squinted up his face at me. "Things pretty bad, Mike?"

"Not so bad they can't get worse."

"Gee."

I left him there fiddling with his distributor. Outside the traffic was thick and fast. Women with bundles were crowding the sidewalks and baby carriages were parked alongside the buildings.

Normal, I thought, a nice normal day. I hauled my heap away from the curb, cut back to Broadway and headed home. It took thirty minutes to get there, another thirty for a quick lunch at the corner and I went into the building fishing my keys out of my pocket.

Any other time I would have seen them. Any other time it would have been dark outside and light inside and my eyes wouldn't have been blanked out. Any other time I would have had a rod on me and it wouldn't have happened so easy. But this was now and not some other time.

They came out of the corners of the lobby, the two of them, each one with a long-nosed revolver in his fist and a yen to use it. They were bright boys who had been around a long time and who knew all the angles. I got in the elevator, leaned against the wall while they patted me down, turned around and faced the door as they pushed the LOBBY button instead of getting off, and walked out in front of them to my car.

Only the short one seemed surprised that I was clean. He didn't like it at all. He felt around the seat while his buddy kept his gun against my neck, then got in beside me.

You don't say much at a time like that. You wait and keep hoping for a break knowing that if it came at all it would be against you. You keep thinking that they wouldn't pop you out in broad daylight, but you don't move because you know they will. New York. This is New York. Something exciting happening every minute. After a while you get used to it and don't pay any attention to it. A gunshot, a backfire, who can tell the difference or who cares. A drunk and a dead man, they both look the same.

The boy next to me said, "Sit on your hands."

I sat on my hands. He reached over, found my keys in my pocket and started the car. "You're a sucker, mac," he said.

The one in the back said, "Shut up and drive." We pulled out into the street and his voice came again. This time it was closer to my ear. "I don't have to warn you about nothing, do I?"

The muzzle of the gun was a cold circle against my skin. "I know the score," I said.

"You only think you do," he told me.

Chapter Nine

I could feel the sweat starting down the back of my neck. My insides were all bottled up tight. My hands got tired and I tried to slide them out and the side of the gun smashed into my head over my ear and I could feel the blood start its slow trickle downward to join the sweat.

The guy at the wheel threaded through Manhattan traffic, hit the Queens Midtown Tunnel and took the main drag out toward the airport. He did it all nice and easy so there wouldn't be any trouble along the way, deliberately driving slowly until I wanted to tell him to get it rolling and quit fooling around. They must have known how I felt because the guy in the back bored the rod into me every time I tightened up and laughed when he did it.

Overhead an occasional plane droned in for a landing and I thought we were going into the field. Instead he passed right by it, hit a stretch where no cars showed ahead and started to let the Ford out.

I said, "Where we going?"

"You'll find out."

The gun tapped my neck. "Too bad you took the car."

"You had a nice package under the hood for me."

The twitch on the wheel was so slight the car never moved, but I caught the motion. For a second even the pressure against my neck stopped.

"Like it?" the driver asked.

He shouldn't have licked his lips. They should have taught him better.

The pitch was right there in my lap and I swung on it hard. "It stunk. I figured the angle and had a mechanic pull it."

"Yeah?"

"So I punch the starter and blooie. It stunk."

This time his head came around and his eyes were little and black, eyes so packed with a crazy terror that they watered. His foot slammed into the brake and the tires screamed on the pavement.

It wasn't quite the way I wanted it but it was just as good. Buster in the back seat came pitching over my shoulder and I had his throat in my hands before he could do a thing about it. I saw the driver's gun come out as the car careened across the road and when it slapped the curbing the blast caught me in the face.

There wasn't any sense holding the guy's neck any more, not with the hole he had under his chin. I shoved as hard as I could, felt the driver trying to reach around the body to get at me while he spit out a string of curses that blended together in an incoherent babble.

I had to reach across the corpse to grab him and he slid down under the wheel still fighting, the rod in his hand. Then he had it out from the tangle of clothes and was getting up at me.

But by then it was too late. Much too late. I had my hand clamped over his, snapped it back and he screamed the same time the muzzle rocketed a bullet into his eyeball and in the second before he died the other eye that was still there glared at me balefully before it filmed over.

They happen fast, those things. They happen, yet time seems to drag by when there's only a matter of seconds and the first thing you wonder is why nobody has come up to see what was going on, then you look down the road and the car you saw in the distance when it all started still hasn't reached you yet, and although two kids across the street are pointing in your direction, nobody else is.

So I got in the driver's side, sat the two things next to me in an upright position and drove back the way we came. I found a cutoff near the airport, turned into it and followed the road until it became a one-lane drive and when I reached its limit there was a sign that read DEAD END.

I was real cute this time. I sat them both under the sign in a nice, natural position and drove back home. All the way back to the apartment I thought of the slobs who gave me credit for finding both gimmicks in the heap and then suddenly realized I was dumber than they figured and the big one was still there ready to go off any second.

Night had seeped in by the time I reached the apartment. I parked and went up to the apartment, opened the door enough to call in for her to take the chain off, but it wasn't necessary at all.

There was no chain.

There was no Lily either and I could feel that cold feeling crawl up my back again. I walked through the rooms to be sure, hoping I was wrong when I was right. She was gone and everything she owned was gone. There wasn't even a hairpin left to show that she had been there and I was so damned mad my eyes squinted almost shut and I was cursing them, the whole stinking pack of them under my breath, cursing the efficiency of their organization and the power they held in reserve, swearing at the way they were able to do things nobody else could do.

I grabbed the phone and dialed Pat's number. Headquarters told me he had left for the day and I put the call through to his apartment. He said hello and knew something was up the minute he heard my voice. "Lily Carver, Pat, you know her?"

"Carver? Damn, Mike . . ."

"I had her here at the apartment and she's gone."

"Where?"

"How am I supposed to know where! She didn't leave here by herself. Look . . ."

"Wait up, friend. You have some explaining to do. Did you know she had been investigated?"

"I know the whole story, that's why I pulled

her out of Brooklyn. She had the city boys, the feds and another outfit on her back. The last bunch pulled a fast one today and got her out of here somehow."

"You stuck your neck out on that one."

"Ah, shut up," I said. "If you have a description, pass it around. She might know what it was the Torn kid was bumped for."

His breathing came in heavy over the receiver. "A pickup went out on her yesterday, Mike. As far as we knew she disappeared completely. I wish to hell you let me in on the deal."

"What have you got on her?" I asked him.

"Nothing. At least not now. A stoolie broke the news that she was to be fingered for a kill."

"Mafia?"

"It checks."

"Damn," I said.

"Yeah, I know how you feel." He paused, then, "I'll keep looking around. There's big trouble winding up, Mike."

"That's right."

"Stuff has been pouring in here."

"Like what?"

"Like more tough guys seen on the prowl. We picked up one on a Sullivan rap already."

I grunted. "That law finally did some good."

"The word is pretty strong. You know what?"

"What?"

"You keep getting mentioned in the wrong places."

"Yeah." I lit up a smoke and pulled in a deep

drag. "This rumble strictly on the quiet between you and me?"

"I told you yes once."

"Good. Anybody find a pair of bodies propped up against a sign in Queens?"

He didn't say anything right away. Then he whispered huskily, "I should've figured it. I sure as blazes should've figured it."

"Well, just don't figure me for your boy. I checked my rod in a few days ago."

"How'd it happen?"

"It was real cute," I said. "Remind me to tell you someday."

"No wonder the boys are out for you."

"Yeah," I said, then I laughed and hung up.

Tonight there'd be more. Maybe a whole lot more.

I stood there and listened and outside the window there was another laugh. The city. The monster. It laughed back at me, but it was the kind of a laugh that didn't sound too sure of itself any more.

Then the phone jangled and the laugh became the muted hum once more as I said hello. The voice I half expected wasn't there. This one was low and soft and just a little bit sad. It said, "Mike?"

"Speaking."

"Michael Friday, Mike."

I could visualize her mouth making the words. A ripe, red mouth, moistly bright, close to the phone and close to mine. I didn't know what to answer her with, except, "Hi, where are you?"

"Downtown." She paused for a moment. "Mike . . . I'd like to see you again."

"Really?"

"Really."

"Why?"

"Maybe to talk, Mike. Would you mind?"

"At one time I would. Not any more."

Her smile must have had the same touch of sadness her voice had just then. "Perhaps I'm using that for an excuse."

"I'd like that better," I said.

"Will you see me then?"

"Just say where and when."

"Well . . . one of Carl's friends is giving a party this evening. I'm supposed to be there and if you don't mind . . . could we go together? We don't have to stay very long."

I thought about it a minute. I let a lot of things run through my mind, then I said, "Okay, I don't have anything else on the fire. I'll meet you in the Astor lobby at ten. How's that?"

"Fine, Mike. Shall I wear a red carnation or something so you'll know me?"

"No . . . just smile, kid. Your mouth is one thing I'll never forget."

"You've never really got close enough to tell."

"I can remember how I said good-bye the last time."

"That isn't *really* close," she said as she hung up.

I looked at the phone when I put it down. It was black, symmetrical and efficient. Just to talk to somebody put a thousand little things into operation and the final force of it all culminated in a minor miracle. You never knew or thought about how it happened until it was all over. Black, symmetrical, efficient. It could be a picture of a hand outlined in ink. Their organization was the same and you never knew the details until it was too late.

That's when they'd like me to see the picture.

When it was too late.

How many tries were there now? The first one they spilled me over the cliff. Then there was laughing boy who kept his gun in his pocket. And don't forget the dead-end sign. That one really must have scared them.

The jerks.

And someplace in the city were two others. Charlie Max and Sugar Smallhouse. For a couple of grand they'd fill a guy's belly with lead and laugh about it. They'd buck the biggest organization in the country because theirs was even bigger. They wouldn't give a damn where they scrammed to because wherever they went their protection went too. The name of the Mafia was magic. The color of cash was even bigger magic.

My lips peeled back over my teeth when I thought of them. Maybe now that they knew about the dead-end sign they'd do a little drinking to calm themselves down. Maybe they'd be thinking if they really were good enough after all. Then they'd decide that they were and wait around until it happened and if it came out right in a penthouse somewhere, or in a crummy dive someplace else one of the kings would swallow hard and make other plans and begin to get curious about footsteps behind him and the people around him. Curiosity that would put knots in their stomach first, tiny lumps that would harden into balls of terror before too long.

Ten o'clock. It was still a few hours off.

Ten o'clock, an exquisite, desirable mouth. Eyes that tried to eat you. Ten o'clock Michael Friday, but I had another appointment first.

I started in the low Forties and picked the spots. They were short stops because I wasn't after a good time. I could tell when I was getting ripe by the sidewise looks that came my way. In one place they started to move away from me so I knew I was nearing the end. A little pigeon I knew shook his head just enough so I knew they weren't there and when his mouth pulled down in a tight smile I could tell he wasn't giving me much of a chance.

Nine fifteen. I walked into Harvey Pullen's place in the Thirties. Harvey didn't want to serve me but I waited him out. He went for the tap and I shook my head and said, "Coke."

He poured it in a hurry, walked away and left me by the faded redhead to drink it. A plain-clothes man I recognized walked in, had a fast beer at the bar, took in the crowd through the back mirror, finished his butt and walked out. In a way I hoped he had spotted me, but if he did he was better at spotting than I was at keeping from being spotted.

She didn't move her mouth at all. Sometimes the things they pick up in stir pay off and this was one of them. She said, "Hammer, ain't 'cha?"

"Uh-huh."

"Long John's place. They're settin' you up."

I sipped my Coke. "Why you?"

"Take a look, buster. Them creeps gimme the business a long time ago. I coulda had a career."

"Who saw them?"

"I just came from there."

"What else?"

"The little guy's a snowbird and he's hopped."

"Coppers?"

"Nobody. Just them. The gang in the dump ain't wise yet."

I laid the Coke down, swirled the ice around in the glass and rubbed out my cigarette. The redhead had a sawbuck on her lap when I left.

Long John's. The name over the door didn't say so, but that's what everybody called it. The bartender had a patch over one eye and a peg leg. No parrot.

A drunk sat on the curb puking into the gutter between his legs. The door was open and you could smell the beer and hear a pair of shrill voices. Background music supplied by a jukebox. Maybe a dozen were lined up at the bar talking loud and fast. The curses and filth sifted out of the conversation like minor high lights and the women's voices shrilled again.

The boys were pros playing it cute.

Sugar Smallhouse was sitting at the corner of the bar, his back facing the door so anybody coming in wouldn't recognize him.

Charlie Max was in the back corner facing the door so anybody coming in he'd recognize.

They played it cute but they didn't play it right and Charlie Max took time out to bend his head into the match he held up to light his cigarette and that's when I came in and stood behind his partner.

I said, "Hello, Sugar," and thought the glass he held would crumple under his fingers. The little hairs on the back of his neck went up straight like happens to a dog when he meets another dog, only on this mutt the skin under the hair had happened to be a pale, pale yellow.

Sugar had heard the word. He had heard other people talk. He knew about the sign marked DEAD END and about me and how things hadn't happened as they were planned. I could feel the things churning through his head as I reached under his arm for rod and all the while Sugar never moved a muscle. It was a little rod with a big bore. I flipped the shells out of the cylinder, dropped them in my pocket and put the gun back in its nest. Sugar didn't get it. He sweated until it soaked through the collar of his shirt but he still didn't get it.

Long John came up, saw me half hidden behind Sugar and said, "What'll it be, feller?" Then Sugar got it while Long John's eye got big and round. I had my hands around his middle in just the right spot, jerked hard and fast with my locked thumbs going into flesh under the breastbone like a kid snapping worms. Hard and fast . . . just once, and Sugar Smallhouse was another drunk who was sleeping it off at the bar.

And Charlie Max was a guy suddenly alive and sober coming up out of his chair trying to clear a gun from a hip holster to collect his bonus. Eternity took place right then in the space of about five seconds of screaming confusion. Somebody saw the gun and the scream triggered the action. Charlie's gun never got quite cleared because the dame beside him pushed too hard getting away and his chair caught him behind the knees. They were all over the joint, cursing, pushing, falling out of the way and fighting to make the door. Then the noise stopped and it was just a tableau of silent panic because the crowd was behind me and there was nothing more to do except stand there with fascinated terror as Charlie Max scrambled for his rod and I closed in with a couple of quick steps.

The gun was there in his fist, coming up and around as I brought my foot up and the things that were in Charlie's face splashed all over the floor. His face looked soft and squashy a second, became something not at all human and he tried once more with the gun.

Nobody heard that kick because his arm made too much noise.

Somehow his eyes were still there, swelling fast, yet still bright. They were eyes that should have been filled with excruciating pain, but horror pushed it out as he saw what was going to happen to him.

"The job was too big, buddy. Somebody should have told you how many guys I put on their backs with skulls split apart because they were gunning for me." I said it real easy and reached for the gun.

The voice behind me said, "Don't touch it, Hammer."

I looked up at the tall guy in the blue pin-striped suit, straightened and grunted my surprise. His face stayed the way it was. There were two more of them standing in the back of the room. One was trying to wake up Sugar Smallhouse. The other came forward, ran his hands over me, looked at his partner with a startled expression that was almost funny before giving me a stare that you might see coming from a kid watching a ballplayer hit a homer.

There wasn't a damn thing they could do and they knew it, so I turned around, walked back outside and started cross-town to the Astor.

Washington had finally showed up.

She was waiting there in a corner of the lobby. There were others who were waiting too and used the time just to watch her. Some had even taken up positions where they could move in if the one she was waiting for didn't show up. She wasn't wearing a red carnation, but she did smile and

I could almost feel that mouth on me across the room.

Her hair was the same swirly mass that was as buoyant as she was. There aren't many words to describe a woman like Michael Friday as she was just then. You have to look at the covers of books and pick out the parts here and there that you like best, then put them all together and you have it. There was nothing slim about her. Maybe a sleekness like a well-fed, muscular cat, an athletic squareness to her shoulders, a sensual curve to her hips, and antagonizing play of motion across her stomach that seemed unconsciously deliberate. She stood there lazily, flexing one smoothly rounded leg that tightened the skirt across her thigh.

I grinned at her and she held out her hand. My own folded around it, stayed there and we walked out together. "Waiting long?" I asked her.

She squeezed my arm under hers. "Longer than I usually wait for anyone. Ten minutes."

"I hope I'm worth it."

"You aren't."

"But you can't help yourself," I finished.

Her elbow poked me. "How did you know?"

"I don't," I said. "I'm just bragging."

There wasn't any smile there now. "Damn you," she whispered. I could feel her go all tight against me, saw her do that trick with her tongue that left her mouth damp and waiting. I pulled my eyes away and opened the door of the cab that sat at the curb, helped her in and climbed in after her.

"Where to?"

She leaned forward, gave an address on Riverside Drive and eased back into the cushions.

It seemed to come slowly, the way sleep does when you're too tired, the gradual coming together of two people. Slow, then faster and all of a sudden her arms were around me and my hands were pressing into her back and my fingers curled in her hair. I looked at that mouth that wasn't just damp now, but wet and she said, "Mike, damn you," softly and I tasted the hunger in her until the fury of it was too much and I let her go.

Some shake and some cry, some even demand right then, but all she did was close her eyes, smile, open them again and relax beside me. I held out a cigarette, lit it for her, did mine and sat there without saying anything until the cab stopped by the building.

When we were in the lobby I said, "What are we supposed to be doing here, gal?"

"It's a party. Out-of-town friends of Carl and his business associates get together."

"I see. Where do you come in?"

"You might call me a greeter. I've always been the go-between for my big brother. You might say . . . he takes advantage of my good looks."

"It's an angle." I stopped her and nodded toward one of the love seats in the corner. She frowned, then went over and sat down. I parked next to her and turned out the light on the table beside me. "You said you wanted to talk. We'll never make it upstairs."

Her fingers made nervous little motions in her

lap. "I know," she said softly. "It was about Carl."

"What about him?"

She looked at me appealingly. "Mike . . . I did what you told me to. I . . . found out all about you."

"So?"

"I . . . it's no use trying to be clever or anything. Carl is mixed up in something. I've always known that." She dropped her eyes to her hands, twining her fingers together. "A lot of people are . . . and it didn't seem to matter much, really. He has all sorts of important friends in government and business. They seem to know what he does so I never complained."

"You just took whatever he gave you without asking," I stated.

"That's right. Without asking."

"Sort of what you don't know won't hurt you."

Michael stared blankly at her lap for a few seconds. "Yes."

"Now you're worried."

"Yes."

"Why?"

The worry seemed to film her eyes over. "Because . . . before it was only legal things that gave him trouble. Carl . . . had lawyers for that. Good ones. They always took care of things." She laid her hand over mine. It shook a little. "You're different."

"Say it."

"I . . . can't."

"All right. You're a killer, Mike. You're dirty,

nasty and you don't care how you do it as long as you do it. You've killed and you'll keep killing until you get killed yourself."

I said, "Just tell me one thing, kid. Are you afraid for me or Carl?"

"It isn't for you. Nothing will ever touch you." She said it with a touch of bitterness that was soft and sad at the same time.

I looked at her wonderingly. "You're not making sense now."

"Mike . . . look at me closely and you'll see. I . . . love Carl. He's always taken care of me. I love him, don't you see? If he's in trouble . . . there are other ways, but not you, Mike, not you. I . . . wouldn't want that."

I took my hand away gently, lit a cigarette and watched the smoke sift out into the room. Michael smiled crookedly as she watched me. "It happened fast, Mike," she said. "It sounds very bad and very inadequate. I'm a very lovely phony, you're thinking and I can't blame you a bit. No matter what I ever say, you'll never believe me. I could try to prove it but no matter how hard I tried or what I did, it would only make it look worse so I won't try any more at all. I'd just like to say this, Mike. I'm sorry it had to be this way. You . . . hit me awfully hard. It never happened to me before. Shall we go up now?"

I got up, let her take my arm and walked to the elevator. She hit the top button and stood there facing the door without speaking, but when I squeezed her arm her hand closed tighter around mine and she tossed her hair back to start the smile she'd have when we got out.

Carl's two boys were by the door in the foyer. They wore monkey suits and on them the term was absolutely descriptive. They started their smiling when they saw Michael and stopped when they saw me. You could see them exchange looks trying to figure the next move and they weren't up to it. We were through the door and a girl was taking my hat while they stood there watching us foolishly.

The place was packed. It was loud with laughs and conversation to the point where the music from the grand piano in the corner barely penetrated. Quiet little men with trays passed through the huddled groups handing out drinks and as heads turned to take them I could spot faces you see in the paper often. Some you saw in the movies too, and there were a few you heard making political speeches over the air.

Important people. So damn important you wondered about the company they kept because in each group were one or two not so important unless you looked at police records or knew what they did for a living.

There were hellos from a dozen different directions. Michael smiled, waved back and started to steer me toward the closest group. Leo Harmody was there in all of his self-assuming importance ready to introduce her to the others. I took my arm away and said, "You go to it, baby. I'll find the bar and get a drink."

163

She nodded, a trace of a frown shadowing the corner of her mouth.

So I went to the bar.

Where Affia was holding Velda's hand and Billy Mist was giving her a snow job while Carl Evello watched cheerfully.

Velda was good. She showed pleasant curiosity and smiled. Carl wasn't so good. He got a little white.

Billy Mist was even worse. He got color in his greasy face but most of it was deep red and his lips tightened so much his teeth showed. I said, "If you're wondering, Carl, your little sister invited me along."

"Oh?"

"Charming girl," I said. "You'd never know she was your sister."

Then I looked at Billy. I was hating his guts inside and out so hard I could hardly stand still. I looked him over real slow like I was trying to find a spot in the garbage pail for the latest load and said, "Hello, stupid."

They can't take it. You can tear their heart out with one word and they can't take it. Billy's face was something ready to blow up like a landmine and he wasn't even thinking of the consequences. He was all alone in the room with me for that brief second and his hand tightened, got ready to grab something under his coat and right at the top of everything he felt I just stood there lazy-like and said, "Go ahead."

And he thought and thought about the dead men

and watched his bubble bust wide open because his mind was telling him he'd never make it while he faced me and he got like Carl. White.

But I wasn't watching Billy Mist any more. I was watching Al Affia, plodding Al Affia who had the waterfront sewed up. Ignorant, thickheaded, slow Al who kept stroking Velda's hand all the while and who didn't turn color or go tight or do anything at all except say, "What's the matter with you guys?"

Velda repeated it. "What *is* the matter? After all . . ."

"Forget it, honey," Billy told her. "Just kidding around. You know how it is."

"Sure you know how it is," Al said.

I looked at the Brooklyn boy and watched him carve his face into a grin, muscle by muscle. Somebody should have mentioned Al's eyes to the boys. They weren't a bit stupid. They were small and close together, but they were bright with a lot of things nobody ever knew about. Someday they'd know.

"Nobody introduced me to the lady," I said.

Carl put his drink down on the bar, afraid to let go of it. "Hammer, I believe it is." He looked at me questioningly and I grinned. "Yes, Mike Hammer. This is Miss Lewis. Candy Lewis."

"Hello, Candy," I said.

"Hello, Mike."

"Neat. Very neat. Model?"

"I do fashions for newspaper advertising."

Good mind, that secretary of mine. Nice and

easy to explain to Billy how come she was shooting it with a couple of newshawks. I wondered how she had smoothed out his feelings.

She knew what I was thinking and went me one better. "What do you do, Mr. Hammer?"

They were watching me now. I said, "I hunt."

"Big game?"

"People," I said, and grinned at Billy Mist.

His nostrils seemed to flare out a little. "Interesting."

"You'll never know, chum. It gets to be real sport after a while." His mouth pressed together, a nasty smirk starting. "Like tonight. I got me two more. You ever hunt?"

His face wasn't red any more. It was calm and deadly. "Yeah, I hunt."

"We ought to try it together sometime. I'll show you a few tricks."

A low rumble came from Al's chest. "I'd like to see that," he laughed. "I sure would."

"Some people haven't got the guts for it," I told him. "It looks easy when you're always on the right side of a gun." I took them all in with one sweep of my eyes. "When you're on the wrong end it gives you the squirms. You know what I mean?"

Carl was on the verge of saying something. I would like to have heard it, but Leo Harmody came up, bowed himself into our little clique with a deep laugh and spoke to Velda. "Could I borrow you long enough to meet a friend of mine, my dear?"

166

"No, certainly not. You don't care, do you, Billy?"

"Go ahead. Bring her back," he told Leo. "We was talking."

She smiled at the four of us, got down off the stool and walked away. Billy wasn't looking at me when he said, "You better stay home nights from now on, wise guy."

I didn't look at him either. I kept watching Velda passing through the crowd. I said, "Any time, any place," and left them there together. A waiter came by with a tray, offered me a drink and I picked one up. It was a lousy drink but I threw it down anyway.

People kept saying hello just to be polite and I said hello back. I picked Michael out of the crowd and saw that she was looking around for me too. Just as I started toward her I heard a whispered, "Mike!"

I stood there, took another drink from a passing waiter and sipped it. Velda said, "Meet me on the corner in an hour. The drug store."

It was enough. I walked off, waved to Michael and waited while she made excuses to her friends.

Her smile looked tired, her face worried, but she swung across the room and held her hands out to me. "Enjoying yourself?"

"Oh, somewhat."

"I saw you talking to my brother."

"And friends. He sure has great friends."

"Is everything . . . all right?"

"For now."

She sucked her lip between her teeth and frowned. "Take me home, Mike."

"Not tonight, kid." Her face came up, hurt. "I've been read off," I said. "I'm unhealthier than ever to be seen with. When it happens I don't want you around."

"Carl?"

"He's part of it."

"And you think I am too."

"Michael, you're a nice kid. You're lovely as hell and you have everything to go with it. If you're trying to get something across to me I don't get it. Even if I did I wouldn't trust you a bit. I could go crazy nuts about you but I still wouldn't trust you. I told you a word the last time I saw you. It was Mafia. It's a word you don't speak right out because it means trouble. It's a word that has all the conniving and murder in the world behind it and as long as it touches you I'm not trusting you."

"You . . . didn't feel that way . . . when you kissed me."

There was no answer to it. I ran my hand along her cheek and squeezed her ear while I grinned at her. "A lot of things don't make much sense. They just happen."

"Will I see you again?"

"Maybe."

She walked to the door with me, said good-by and let her tongue run over her mouth slowly like she was enjoying the taste of something. I grabbed my hat and got out of there fast before she talked me into something I wasn't going to get talked into.

The two goons were still outside. There was something set in their faces and they didn't move when I went past them. When the elevator came up I stepped in, hit the button marked B and had a smoke on the way down. The door opened, I hit the main-floor buzzer as I got out and the elevator went back up a floor.

It wasn't hard to get out of there the back way. I went past the furnaces, angled around closed storerooms and found the door. There was a concrete yard in back bordered by a fence with a door that swung into the same arrangement on the other side. This time I met a young kid firing one of the furnaces, held out a bill as I went by and said, "Dames. You know how it is." He nodded wisely, speared the bill and went back to his work whistling.

I found the drug store and went in for a soda. They sold magazines up front so I brought one back with me while I waited. It was five minutes past the hour when Velda came in, saw me and slipped into the booth.

"You get around, Mike."

"I was thinking of saying the same to you. How come you tangled with Mist?"

"Later. Now listen, I haven't too much time. Earlier this evening two names came up. One of Carl's men turned in a report and I was close enough to hear it. The report was that somebody had double checked on Nicholas Raymond and Walter McGrath. Carl got all excited about it.

"At the time I was talking to Al and Billy and had my back to Carl. He sent the guy off, called Billy off and I could tell from Billy's face that he passed the news on to him. He looked like a dead fish when he came back to the bar with us. He was so mad his hands were shaking."

I said, "Did Affia get the news?"

"Most likely. I excused myself for a few minutes to give him a chance to pass it politely."

"I wonder about something, Kitten."

"What?"

"I made a few phone calls."

"It sounded more important than that."

"Maybe Washington is getting hot."

"They'll have to get hotter," Velda grinned. "Billy said he had to talk a little business to-night." She reached in her handbag and brought out something. "He gave me a key to his apart-ment and told me to go ahead up and wait for him there."

I whistled between my teeth and picked the key out of her fingers. "Let's go then. This is hot."

"Not me, Mike. You go." There was a deadly seriousness about her face.

"What's the rest of it, Velda?"

"This is a duplicate key I dragged Carlo Barnes out of bed to make up for me. It took some fast and fancy working to get it so quickly."

"Yeah."

"Al Affia caught the pitch and invited me up to his place for awhile *before* I went to Billy's," Velda said softly.

"The lousy little . . ."

"Don't worry about it, Mike."

"I'm not. I'm just going to smash his face in for him, that's all." I sat there with my hands making fists and the hate pumping through my veins so hard it hurt.

Velda squeezed my hand and dumped a small aspirin bottle out of her bag and showed it to me. There weren't any pills in it, only a white powder. "Chloral," she said. "Don't worry."

I didn't like it. I knew what she figured to do and I didn't go for the play. "He's no tourist. The guy's been around."

"He's still a man."

My mouth felt dry. "He's a cagey guy."

Her elbow nudged her side meaningly. "I still have that, Mike."

You have to do things you don't want to do sometimes. You hate yourself for it but you still have to do it. I nodded, said, "Where's his place?"

"Not Brooklyn. He has a special little apartment under the name of Tony Todd on Forty-seventh between Eighth and Ninth Avenues." She pulled a note pad out, jotted down the number with the phone to go with it and handed it over. "Just in case, Mike."

I looked at it, memorized every detail there, then let the flame of my lighter wipe it out of existence. My beautiful, sleek animal was smiling at me, her eyes full of excitement and when you looked hard you could see the same thing there that you could see in mine. She stood up, winked and said,

"Good hunting, Mike."

Then she was gone.

I gave her five minutes. I followed the shadows further uptown along the Drive to the building Billy Mist owned.

For the first time I was glad he was such a big man. He was so damn big he didn't have to stake anybody out around his place. He could relax in the luxury of security knowing that just one word could bring in an army if anybody tried to take the first step across the line.

It was another one of those things that came easy. You go in like you belonged there. You get on the elevator and nobody notices. You get off and go down the hall then stick the key in the lock and the door opens. You get treated to the best that money can buy even if the taste is crummy.

There were eight rooms in all. They were spotlessly clean and treated with all the care a well-paid maid could give them. I took forty-five minutes going through seven of them without finding one thing worth looking at until I came to the eighth.

It was a little room off the living room. At one time it must have been intended for a storeroom, but now it had a TV set, a tilt-back chair with an ottoman in place facing it, a desk and a bookcase loaded with pulps. Out of eight rooms here was the place where Billy Mist spent his solo time.

The desk was locked, but it didn't take more than a minute to get it open. Right in the middle section was a dimestore scrapbook fat with clippings and photos and he was in all of them. My greasy little friend was one hell of an egotist from the looks of the thumbmarks on the pages.

Another ten minutes went by going through the book and then I came to Berga's picture. There was no caption. It was just a rotogravure cutout and Billy was grinning at the camera. Berga was supposed to be background but she outsmiled Billy. Two pages later she came up again only this time she was with Carl Evello and it was Billy who was in the background talking to somebody hidden by Carl's back. I found two more like that, first with Billy, then with Carl, and topping it all was a close-up glossy of Berga at her best with *"love to my Handsome Man"* penned in white across the bottom.

Nothing else unless you wanted to count the medicine bottles in the pigeonholes. It looked like the cabinet in the bathroom. Billy must have had a pretty nervous stomach.

I closed the desk, locked it and wiped it clean. I went back to the living room, checked my watch and knew the time was getting close. I picked up the phone and dialed Pat's home number. Nobody answered so I called headquarters and that's where he was. It was a tired, disgusted Pat that said hello.

"Busy, Pat?"

"Yeah, up to my ears. Where have you been? I've been calling between your office and your house all night."

"If I told you you'd never believe it. What's up?"

"Plenty. Sugar Smallhouse talked."

I could feel the chills crawl up my legs until the hairs on the backs of my hands stood straight out.

"Give, Pat. What's the score?"

He lowered his voice deliberately and didn't sound like himself at all. "Sugar was on the deal when Berga got bumped. Charlie Max was called in on the job but didn't make it."

"Come on, come on. Who did he finger?"

"He didn't. The other faces were all new to him."

"Damn it," I exploded, "can't you get something out of him?"

"Not any more, pal. Nobody can. They were taking the two downtown to the D.A.'s and somebody chopped them."

"What're you talking about?"

"Sugar and Charlie are dead. One Federal man and one city cop are shot up pretty bad. They were sprayed by a tommy gun from the back seat of a passing car."

"Capone stuff. Hell, this isn't prohibition. For Pete's sake, Pat, how big are these guys? How far can they go?"

"Pretty far, it looks like. Sugar gave us one hot lead to a person with a Miami residence. He's big, too."

I could taste something sour in my mouth. "Yeah," I said, "so now he'll be asked polite questions and whatever answers he gives will satisfy them. I'd like to talk to the guy. Just him and me and a leather-covered sap. I'd love to hear his answers."

"It doesn't work that way, Mike."

"For me it does. Any trace of the car?"

"Sure, we found it." He sounded very tired. "A stolen job and the gun was still in it. We traced it to a group heisted from an armory in Illinois. No prints. Nothing. The lab is working on other things."

"Great. A year from now we'll get the report. I'd like to do it my way."

"That's why I was calling you."

"Now what."

"That screwball play of yours with Sugar and Max. The feds are pretty sore about it."

"You know what to tell them," I said.

"I did. They don't want to waste time pulling you out of jams."

"Why, those apple heads! Who are they supposed to be kidding? They must have had a tail on me all night to run me down in that joint and they sure waited until it was finished before they came in to get their suits dirty."

"Mike . . ."

"Nuts to them, brother. They can stick their heads . . ."

"Shut up for a minute, will you!" Pat's voice was a low growl. "You didn't have a tail . . . those two hoods did. They lost the boys and didn't get picked up again until they reached Long John's."

"So what?"

"So they needed a charge to drag them in on. The boys caught the tail, ditched their rods some-

175

place and when one of our plain clothes men braced them they were clean. They had a second tail and didn't know it, but they didn't take any chances and pulled some pretty fancy footwork just in case. If they could have been pulled in on a Sullivan rap we would have squeezed something out of them. You didn't leave them in condition to talk."

"Tell 'em thanks," I grunted. "I don't like to be gunned for. I'll try not to break up their next play."

"Yeah," Pat said sourly.

"Anything on Carver yet?" I asked him.

"Not a thing. We have two freshly killed blondes, more or less. One's been in the river at least three days and the other was shot by an irate lover just tonight. They interest you?"

"Quit being funny." I looked at my watch. Time was getting too damn short. I said, "I'll buzz you if anything turns up, otherwise I'll see you in the morning."

"Okay. Where are you now?"

"In the apartment of a guy named Billy Mist and he's due in any second."

His breath made a sharp hissing sound over the phone as I hung up.

I had almost timed it too close. The elevator marker was climbing toward the floor when I reached it and just in case I stepped around the corner of the stairs, went up to the first landing and waited.

Billy Mist and a heavyset muscleman came off the elevator, opened the apartment door and went

176

in. There wasn't anything I wanted to talk to him about so I took the stairs back down instead of the elevator and got out the front door in one piece.

I got halfway down the block when some elusive little thing flashed across my mind and my eyes twisted into a squint as I tried to catch it. Something little. Something trivial. Something in the apartment I should have noticed and didn't. Something that screamed out to be seen and I had passed it by. I tried to bring it into focus and it wouldn't come and after a minute or so it passed out of sight altogether.

I stood there on the corner waiting for the light and a taxi swung by. I had the briefest glimpse inside the back and I saw Velda sitting there with somebody else. I couldn't stop it and I couldn't chase it. I had to stand there and think about it until I was all mixed up and I wasn't going to feel right until I knew the score. An empty cab came along and I told him to take me down to Forty-seventh Street.

The house was in the middle of the block. It was a beat-up affair fifty years old bearing the scars only a neighborhood like that can give it. The doorbell position said Todd lived on the ground floor in back. I didn't have to do any ringing because the front door was open. The hall was littered with junk I had to push aside until I came to the door that had *Todd* written on the card in the square metal holder.

I didn't have to ring any bells here either. This door was open too. I shoved it open and the light streamed out around me, light that glistened off the fetid pools of vomit on the floor, shining even more ominously from the drops of blood between the pools. The blood was in the hall too, and the light picked it up. It made sticky sounds on the soles of my shoes.

With a rod in my hand I would have felt better. It's company that can do your talking for you and a voice they listen to. I missed the rod, but I went in anyway but on my toes ready to move if I had to.

Nothing happened.

But I saw what had happened.

The glasses were there on the table with a half-empty bottle of mixer and an almost empty fifth of whisky. Ice had melted in the bowl with a few small pieces floating on top of the water.

On the floor was the remains of a milk bottle and there was blood all over one piece. Velda had given him the chloral treatment and he went out, but somehow he had spilled it out of his system and made a play for her. He would have killed her if he could have but she got him with the milk bottle.

Then it hit me all at once and I felt like adding to the pools on the floor. She had gone about in her search, left for Billy's and Al snapped out of it. He didn't stay cold as she had expected him to and Al would have got the news to him by now.

I made a grab for the phone in the corner, spun the dial to Pat's number again and sweated until he answered. I said, "Listen fast, Pat, and no questions. They got Velda. She went up to Billy Mist's place and walked into a trap. Get a squad car up there as fast as you can. Got that? Get her the hell out of there no matter what happens and be damn fast about it because they may be working her over." I shot my number to him and told him to call back as soon as word came through.

When I hung up I was cold with sweat and tasting the cotton in my mouth. I closed the door and hoped Al would come back so I could do things to him myself. I didn't move out of the room until I got impatient waiting for the phone to ring, then I prowled through the place.

There was a full cabinet of liquor I was going to try but the smell of it sickened me when I got the bottle near my mouth so I shoved it back again. *Damn it, I thought, why doesn't he call!*

I started a butt going, spit it out after a second drag and went around the place some more. To keep my mind still and the buzzing out of my ears I used my eyes and saw why Al kept the place at all. For what he wanted it was a pretty good base of operation. There were souvenirs all over the place. It was a sloppy hovel, but sloppiness was part of the setup and probably nobody complained.

Al must have even done a little work there when he was finished with his parties. There were work sheets and union reports spread out on the table and a batch of company check stubs in the drawer held together by a rubber band. Like a sap he

179

left a pair of empty checkbooks in the same drawer and the hundred and fifty he made a week from the company wouldn't have backed up the withdrawals shown in the books.

So he had a sideline. He cheated the government most likely. Try to find whose name the checking account was in and there'd be fun.

The phone still didn't ring so I rolled a stack of blueprints that showed dock layouts. At least two of them did. Nine of the others were ships' plans that were blown up in detail until they centered around one mass of lines I couldn't make out. I threw them all back on the table and started to walk away as the phone rang.

I caught it before the ring was finished and Pat said, "You Mike?"

"Speaking."

"What're you pulling, kid?"

"Cut the funny stuff, Pat, what happened?"

"Nothing, except a pair of my men are highly squiffed off. Mist was in bed alone. He let the cops in, let them look around, then chewed the hell out of them for pulling a search. He made one phone call and I've been catching it ever since."

I wasn't hearing him. I laid the phone back on its rack and stared at it dumbly. It started to ring again. It went through the motions four times, then stopped.

Outside it had started to rain. It tapped the windows in the back of the room, cutting streaks through the dust. When I looked again the dust was gone completely and the window seemed to have a live wavy motion about it. I pulled the Luckies out of my pocket, lit one and watched the smoke. It floated lazily in the dead air, then slowly followed a draft that crossed the room.

I was thinking things that scared me.

My watch counted off the seconds and each tick was louder and more demanding, screaming not to be wasted.

I went back to the table, unfolded the blueprints, pushed the first two aside and looked at the legend on the bottom of the nine others.

The ship's name was there. Same ship. The name was *Cedric*.

It was starting to hang together now. When it was too late it was starting to hang together.

They wouldn't kill her yet, I thought. They'd do a lot of things, but they wouldn't kill her until they were sure. They couldn't afford the chance.

Then when they were sure they'd kill her.

Chapter Ten

I slept hard. The rain on the windows kept me asleep and I went through the morning and the rest of the day with all the things I pictured going through my mind and when they came together in one final, horrible ending I woke up. It was nearly six in the evening but I felt better. Time was too important to waste but I couldn't afford to let it pass while I was half out on my feet.

There was a box of frozen shrimp in the refrigerator I put on the fire and while it cooked up I put through a call. It took two more to locate Ray Diker and his voice sounded as sharp and pinched as his face. He said, "Glad you called, Mike. I was going to buzz you."

"Got something?"

"Maybe. I followed up on Kawolsky. The office he worked for pulled out the records and I got the details. He was hired to cover the Torn kid. She complained that someone was following her and she was a pretty scared baby. She paid the fee in cash and they put Lee on permanent duty. He picked her up in the morning and took her home at night."

"You told me that already, Ray."

"I know, but here's the good part. Lee Kawolsky quit reporting to the office in person after a week of it. He started checking in by phone. The office got ideas about it and put another man outside the apartment and found out Lee was pulling a voluntary twenty-four-hour duty. He was staying with the dame all the time."

"The office complain?"

"What for? It was his business and if she wanted it that way why sound off on it. Her checks still rolled in."

"Did they leave it that way?"

"There wasn't much they could do. The report the other investigator sent in said Lee was doing a fairly serious job of bodyguarding. He had already got into a couple of scrapes over her and she seemed to like it."

It was another thread being woven into place. The rope was getting longer and stronger.

Ray said, "You still there?"

"I'm still here."

"What did you call me for then?"

"The driver of the truck who killed Lee. Got that too?"

"Sure. Harvey Wallace. He lives upstairs over Pascale's saloon on Canal Street. You know where the place is."

"I know," I said.

"Might have something here on Nick Raymond."

"What?"

"He retailed imported tobacco through a concern in Italy. He had his name changed from Raymondo to Raymond before the war. Made a few trips back and forth every year. One of his old customers I ran down said he didn't look like much, but he spent the winters in Miami and dropped a wad of cabbage at the tables there. He was quite a ladies' man too."

"Okay, Ray. Thanks a lot."

"Got a story yet?"

"Not yet. I'll tell you when."

I hung up and turned the shrimp over in the pan. When they were done I ate, finished my coffee and got dressed.

Just as I was going out the front-door buzzer went off and when I opened it the super was standing there with his face twisted up into one big worry and he said, "You better come downstairs, Mr. Hammer."

Whatever it was he didn't want to speak about in the hall and I didn't ask him. I followed him down, got into his apartment and he motioned with his thumb and said, "In there."

She was sitting on the couch with the super's wife wiping the tears away from her face, filthy dirty and her clothes torn and dust streaked.

I said, "Lily!" and she looked up. Her eyes were red things that stared back at me like a rabbit cornered in its hole.

"You know her, Mr. Hammer?"

"Hell yes, I know her." I sat on the couch beside her and felt her hair. It was greasy with dirt, its

184

luster completely gone. "What happened, kid?"

The eyes filled with tears again and her breath came in short, jerky sobs.

"Let her alone a little bit, Mr. Hammer. She'll be all right."

"Where'd you find her?"

"In the cellar. She was holed up in one of the bins. I never would've seen her if I didn't see the milk bottles. First-floor tenants were squawking about somebody stealing their milk. I seen those two bottles and looked inside the bin and there she was. She said to call you."

I took her hand and squeezed it in mine. "You all right? You hurt or anything?"

She licked her lips, sobbed again and shook her head slowly.

The super's wife said, "She's just scared. Supposing I get her cleaned up and into some fresh clothes. She had a bag with her."

White outlined the red of Lily's eyes. She pulled back, her face tight. "No . . . I . . . I'm all right. Let me alone, please let me alone!" Then there was something fierce about the way she looked at me and bit out, "Mike . . . take me with you. Please. Take me with you!"

"She in trouble, Mr. Hammer?"

I looked at him steadily. "Not the kind of trouble you know about."

He saw what I meant, spoke rapidly to his wife in that language of his and her wise little eyes agreed.

"Help me get her upstairs."

The super took her bag, hooked one arm under hers and she came up from the couch. We used the service elevator in the rear, made my floor without meeting anybody and got her inside the apartment.

He said, "Anything I can do to help, just let me know."

"Right. Clam up about this. Tell your wife the same."

"Sure, Mr. Hammer."

"One other thing. Get me a damn big barrel bolt and slap it on my door."

"First thing tomorrow." He closed the door and I locked it after him.

She sat there in the chair like a kid waiting to be slapped. Her face was drawn and the eyes in it were as big as saucers. I fixed her a drink, made her take it all and filled it up again.

"Feel better?"

"A . . . little."

"Want to talk?"

Her teeth were a startling contrast to her skin when she bit her lip and nodded.

"From the beginning," I said.

"They came back," she said. Her voice was so low I could barely hear it. "They tried the door and one of them did something with the lock. It . . . opened. I sat there and I couldn't even scream. I couldn't move. The . . . the chain on the door stopped them." A shudder went through her whole body.

"They were arguing in whispers outside about

the chain, then they closed the door and went away. One of them said they'd need a saw. I . . . couldn't stay here, Mike. I was terrified. I threw my clothes in the bag and ran out but when I got to the street I was afraid they might still be watching and I went down the cellar! Mike . . . I'm . . . I'm sorry."

"That's all right, Lily. I know how it is. Did you see them?"

"No. No, Mike."

The shudder racked her body again and she bit into her finger.

"When . . . that man found me . . . I thought he was . . . one of them."

"You don't have to worry any more, Lily. I'm not going to leave you here alone again. Look, go in and clean up. Take a nice hot bath and fix your hair. Then get something in your stomach."

"Mike . . . are you . . . going out?"

"For a little while. I'll have the super's wife stay with you until I get back. Would you mind that?"

"You'll hurry back?"

I nodded that I would and picked up the phone. The super's wife said she'd be more than glad to help out and would come right up.

From in back of me Lily said, "I'm so dirty. Ask her to bring some rubbing alcohol, Mike."

She said she'd do that too and hung up. Lily had finished her drink and lay with her head against the back of the chair watching me sleepily. The tautness had left her cheeks and color had

187

come back to her mouth. She looked like a dog who had just been lost in the swamp then suddenly found his way home.

I started the water in the tub, filled it and lifted her out of the chair. She was light in my arms, completely relaxed, her breathing soft against my face. There was something too big in her eyes while she was so close to me and the strain of it showed in the corner of her mouth. She dug her fingers into my arms with a repressed hunger of a sort, sucked in her breath in a series of almost soundless staccato jerks and before I could kiss her she twisted her head and buried it against my shoulder.

The super's wife came in while she was still splashing around in the tub. She made clucking noises like a mother hen and wanted to go right to her, but the door was locked so she started scrounging some chow up in the kitchen. The bottle of alcohol was on the table and before I left I knocked on the door.

"You want a rubdown, Lily?"

The water stopped splashing.

"Glad to give you a hand if you want," I said.

She laughed from inside and I felt better. I left the bottle by the door, told the mother hen I was leaving and got.

Seven thirty-two. The gray overcast brought a premature dusk to the city, a gloomy wet shroud that came down and poured itself inside your clothes. It was the kind of night that made the city withdraw into itself, leaving the sidewalks empty and people inside the glass-fronted stores staring aimlessly into the wet.

I left my car where it was and hopped a cab down to Canal. He let me out at Pascale's and I went in the door on the right of the place. Here the hall was clean, clear and well lit. You could hear the hum of voices from the gin mill through the walls, but it diminished as I went up the stairs.

She was a short woman, her hair neatly in place with a ready smile that said hello.

"Mrs. Wallace?"

"Yes."

"My name is Hammer. I'd like to talk to your husband if he's home."

"Certainly. Won't you come in?"

She stepped aside, closed the door and called out, "Harv, there's a gentleman here to see you."

From inside a paper rustled and kids' voices piped up. He said something to them and they quieted down. He came out to the kitchen with that expression one stranger has for another stranger, nodded to his wife, then to me and stuck out his hand.

"Mr. Hammer," his wife said and smiled again. "I'll go in with the children if you'll excuse me."

"Sit down, Mr. Hammer." He pulled a chair out by the table, waved me into it and took one himself. He was one of those big guys with beefy shoulders and thinning hair. There was Irish in his face and a trace of Scandinavian.

"This'll be quick," I told him. "I'm an inves-

189

tigator. I'm not digging up anything unpleasant just for the fun of it and what you say won't go any further."

His tongue rolled around his cheek and he nodded.

"Sometime ago you drove the truck that killed a man named Lee Kawolsky."

The side of his face moved.

"I explained . . . "

"You don't get the angle yet," I said. "Wait. As far as you were concerned it was an out-and-out accident. Your first. It was one of those things that couldn't be helped so you weren't touched for it."

"That's right."

"Okay. Like I said, it's been a long time since it happened. Nobody else but you saw it. Tell me, have you ever gone over the thing in your mind since?"

Harvey said very quietly, "Mr. Hammer . . . there are some nights when I never get to sleep at all."

"You could see the thing happen. Sometimes the details would be sharp, then they'd fade?"

He squinted his eyes at me. "Something like that."

"What are you uncertain about?"

"You know something, Mr. Hammer?"

"Maybe."

This time he leaned forward, his face set in a puzzled grimace. "It's not clear. I see the guy coming out from behind the L pillar and I'm yelling at him while I slam on the brakes. The load in the truck lets go and rams the wall back of the cab and I can feel the wheels . . ." He stopped and looked down at his hands. "He came out too fast. He didn't come out walking."

Harvey looked at me, his eyes beseeching. "You know what I mean? I'm not making up excuses."

"I know," I said.

"I came out of the cab fast and he was under the axle. I know I yelled for somebody to help me. Sometimes . . . I think I remember a guy running. Away, though. Sometimes I think I remember that and I can't be sure."

I stood up and put my hat on. "You can stop worrying then. It wasn't an accident." His eyes came wide open. "It was murder. Kawolsky was pushed. You were the sucker."

I opened a door, waved a finger at him. "Thanks for the help."

"Thank . . . you, Mr. Hammer."

"It's over with so there's no use fooling with the report," I said.

"No . . . but it's good to know. I won't be waking up in the middle of the night any more now."

Ten minutes after nine. In the lobby of the hotel a row of empty telephone booths gaped at me. Two people were sitting in the far corner holding hands. One other, not looking as though he belonged there, was reading the paper and dripping water all over the floor.

The girl at the magazine counter changed a buck

191

into dimes for me and I took the end booth on the row.

Thirty cents got me my party. His voice was deep and fat and it never sounded right coming out of the skinny little neck. He'd need a shave and his suit pressed but he didn't give a damn for either. He was strictly a nobody up until the squash was put on bookie operations then all of a sudden he was a somebody. He had a mind like a recording machine and was making hay in the new deal of black-market betting operations.

I said, "Dave?"

"Right here."

"Mike Hammer."

The voice got closer to the phone and almost too casual. I could see him with his hand cupped around the mouthpiece and his eyes watching everybody in the place. "Sure, boy, what'cha doin'?"

"They're saying things along the row, Dave?"

"Piling up, big boy. Everybody got it."

"How do you feel about it?"

"Come on, mister, you know better'n that." The meaning sifted out of his words and I grinned. There was no humor in the grin.

I said, "I got what they want, kid. You tell it in the right places."

"You're killing me. Try again."

"So you saw me. I was in the bag and let it slip."

His voice dropped an octave. "Look, I'll do a lot of things, but you don't mess with them monkeys. They make a guy talk. Me, I got a big mouth when I get hurt up."

"It'll set, Dave. This is a big one. If it was a little one I'd ask somebody else. They got Velda. Understand that?"

He said three sharp, nasty curses at the same time. "You're trading."

"I'm willing. If it don't come off I'll blow the thing apart."

"Okay, Mike. I'll spin it. Don't bother calling me again, okay?"

"Okay," I said and hung up.

I walked over to the desk and the clerk smiled, "Room, sir?"

"Not now, thanks. I'd like to see the manager."

"I'm afraid you can't. He's gone for the evening. You see . . ."

"He live here?"

"Why, er . . . why, yes, but . . ."

I let a bill do the talking. The guy was well-dressed but underpaid and the ten looked big. "No trouble. I have to speak to him. He won't know."

The bill left my fingers magically. "Suite 101." He pointed a long forefinger across the room. "Take the stairs past the mezzanine. It's quicker."

There was a buzzer beside the door. I leaned on it until I heard the knob turn and a middle-aged, sensitive Latin face was peering out at me. The professional smile creased his lower jaw pulling the thin mustache tighter and he cocked his head in an attentive attitude ready to hear my complaint. His eyes were telling me that he trusted it would be a good one because Mr. Carmen Trivago was preparing to leave in a moment for a very important engagement.

I gave him a shove that wiped the smile clean off his face and he stumbled back inside while I closed the door. There was an instantaneous flash of mingled terror and hatred in his expression that dissolved into indignation as he drew himself up stiffly and said, "What is the meaning of this?"

"Get back inside."

"I . . ."

My hand cracked him across the mouth so hard he hit the wall, flattened against it making unintelligible noises in his throat. He wasn't so stiff when I gave him a shove into the living room. He was all loose and jelly-like as if his bolts were ready to come apart.

I said, "Turn around and look at me." He did. "I'm going to ask you things and you answer them right. If you think you'd do better by lying look at my face and you won't lie. Let me catch you in one and I'll mangle you so damn bad you won't even crawl out of this dump for a month. Just for the hell of it I ought to do something to you now so you know I'm not kidding about it."

Carmen Trivago couldn't stand up any more. His knees went as watery as his eyes and he slumped crookedly on the edge of a chair.

"No . . . don't . . ."

"His right name was Nicholas Raymondo. With an 'O'. You were the only one who knew that. I thought it was your accent, but you knew his name, didn't you?"

His mouth opened to speak but the words wouldn't come out. He nodded dumbly.

"Where'd he get his dough?"

The spread of his hands said he didn't know and before he could shake his head to go with it I rocked him with another open-handed slap that left the prints of my fingers across his jaw.

He couldn't take anything at all and tried to burrow into the chair while he moaned, "Please. No . . . I tell you . . . anything. Please."

"When, then?"

"He had . . . the business. From abroad he . . ."

"I know about that. Business didn't give him the kind of money he spent."

"Yes, yes. It is true. But he never said. He spoke of big things but he never said . . ."

"He liked dames."

Carmen's eyes told me he didn't get what I was driving at.

I said slowly, "So do you. Two of a kind, you guys. Lady killers. You knew his right name. Those things only come when you know a person. You know that much and you know a lot more. Think about it. I'll give you a minute. Just one."

His neck seemed to stretch out of shape as he held his head up. The longer he looked at me the more he curled up inside and his mouth started to move. "It is true . . . he had the money. It was enough. He was . . . satisfied to spend it all on much foolishness. There would be more soon, he told me, much more. At first . . . I thought he was making a boast. But no. He was serious. Never would he tell me more than that."

I took a slow step a little closer to him.

His hands went up to hold me off. "It is true, I swear it! This other money . . . several times when he was feeling, how you say it, high? he would ask me how I would like to have two million dollars. It was always the same. Two million dollars. I would ask how to get it and would smile. Raymondo . . . he had it, I know he had it. I tell you, this money was no good. I knew it would happen someday. I knew . . . "

"How?"

This time his eyes made passes around me, looking for something that wasn't there yet. "Before he . . . died . . . there were men. I knew of these men."

"Say the word."

It almost stuck in his throat, but he managed it. "Mafia," he said hoarsely.

"Did Raymondo know he was being followed?"

"I do not think so."

"You didn't tell him?"

He looked at me as if I was crazy.

"You never thought he was killed accidentally either, did you?" The fear showed in his face so plain it was a voice by itself. "You knew the score right along," I said.

"Please . . ."

"You're a crummy little bastard, Trivago. There's a lot of dead people lying around because you made them that way."

"No, I . . . "

"Shut up. You could have sounded off."

"No!" He stood up, his hands claws that dangled at his sides. "I know them! From Europe I know them and who am I to speak against them. You do not understand what they do to people. You . . . "

My knuckles cracked across his jaw so hard he went back over the arm of the chair and spilled in a heap on the floor. He lay there with his eyes wide open and the spit dribbling out of his open mouth started to turn pink. He was the bug caught in the web trying to hide from the spider and he backed into the hornet's nest.

Carmen Trivago would never be the same again.

I used the phone in the lobby again. I buzzed my apartment and the super's wife answered it. I hadn't told her not to do so, she was doing me a favor. I told her it was me, asked if everything was okay and she said it was. Lily was asleep with the door locked but she could hear her breathing and talking in there. Her husband was making doubly sure things stayed quiet by pretending to do some work in the hall outside.

There were three other phone calls. A Captain Chambers had called and wanted to see me right away. I thanked her and hung up.

I turned up the collar of my trench coat and stepped out into the rain. The wind was lashing it up the street in waves now, pounding it against the buildings and as the cars went by you had a quick look at the drivers as the wipers ripped it aside before the faces muddled into a liquid haze.

The cab didn't wait to be called. He pulled into the curb and I hopped in, gave him the address and stuck a smoke in my mouth.

Someplace Velda was looking at the rain. It wouldn't be a pleasant sound, not this time. She'd be crazy with fear, scared so hard she wouldn't be able to think. They weren't the kind you could stall. She could only wait. And hope.

And someplace the people who had her were thinking too. They were thinking of a long string of kills and two fresh ones propped up against a dead-end sign. They were thinking of the word that went out and before they'd do anything at all they'd think harder still and it wouldn't be until I was dead that they'd feel right to do what they wanted to her.

I wasn't the cops and I wasn't the feds. I was one guy by himself but I was one who could add to the score without giving a damn at all. I was the one guy they were afraid of because the trail of dead men hadn't stopped yet. It was a trail that had to be walked and they were afraid of stepping on it.

Pat was in his office. You had to look twice to make sure he wasn't asleep, then you saw the light glinting off his almost-closed eyes and saw the movement of his mouth as he sucked on the dry pipe.

I threw my hat on the desk and sat down. He

didn't say anything. I got out my next-to-last Lucky, held a light to it and let the smoke go. He still didn't say anything. I didn't have the time to trade thoughts. "Okay, chum, what is it?"

The pipe came out of his mouth slowly. "You conned me, Mike."

I started to get warm all over, an angry flush that burned into my chest. "Great. Just like that I gave you the business! You don't say anything . . . you sit there like a dummy then pull the cork. Say what's eating you or I'll get the hell out of here."

What distrust was in his face turned uncertain. "Mike, this thing is a bombshell. The biggest staff that ever operated on one case is out there working. They're going night and day looking for the answer then you come up with it ready to trade off for something."

I sat back in the chair. I took a deep, relieved pull on the smoke and grinned. "Thanks for the compliment. I didn't know it would get back so fast. Where'd you pick it up?"

"Every stoolie we know has his ears open. What are you trading for?"

My grin pulled tight at the edges, flattened across my teeth and stayed that way. "Velda. The bastards have Velda. She suckered Al Affia into a trap that didn't work and got caught in one herself. She played it too smart and now they have her."

It was quiet in the room. The clock on the wall hummed over the drone of the rain outside, but that was all.

"You don't look too worked up about it," Pat said. Then he saw my eyes and took it back without saying so out loud.

"They'll want to be sure. They'll want to know if I have it or not before they cut loose on her. They'll have to be sure. Right in the beginning they thought Berga Torn passed it on to me, went through my apartment. If it was anybody else they could have taken it easy, but not with me. They knew what was going to happen."

"Let's have it, Mike."

"The answer?" I said. I shook my head. "I don't have it. Not where I can reach out and touch it yet. I need more details."

"So do we. I thought we were sharing this thing."

"I didn't forget. What have you got?"

Pat stared at me a long time, reached out and fanned a few papers across his desk. "Berga didn't escape from the sanitarium. She had it planned for her. She had a guest early that evening, a woman. The name and address were phony and we got no description except that she had brown hair. An attendant stated that she was pretty nervous after the guest left."

I cut in with, "How come you're just finding this stuff out?"

"It's a private sanitarium and they were afraid of ruining their reputation. They held off until we scared them. Anyway, we checked everybody in the place that night and came up with a spot from a couple of female visitors in the next room.

"When the closing bell rang they stood outside in the hall a few minutes talking. They were close to Berga's door and overheard a voice saying . . ." He glanced down at the sheet and read from it. ". . . 'they're after you. They were at the house today.' " The rest of it we had to put together and when we had it the dame was telling her something about the main gate, to be as casual as possible, and there would be a car waiting for her at the northwest corner."

Pat stopped and tapped the sheet. He tapped the stem of the pipe against his teeth and said, "On that corner was an F.B.I. wagon so whoever was waiting had to take up another spot. She got scared out of the deal and started hitchhiking when she didn't see the person she was expecting."

I said, "She saw the person, all right. He was in another car. She knew damn well she was being followed."

"There's something wrong," Pat said.

"Yeah. Like murders on the books as accidents."

Pats jaw worked. "Proof?"

"No, but that's the way it happened." I couldn't see his face, but I knew what he was thinking. In his own way he had covered every detail I had. "The first one was Nicholas Raymond. That's where the answer is, Pat."

His eyes peered out at me. "Nicholas Raymond was a Mafia agent. He ran an import business as an excuse to make frequent overseas trips."

I didn't answer so he said, ". . . He was the guy who ran the stuff into this country that was

201

turned into cash for Mafia operations."

He was watching me so closely that you couldn't see anything but the black pupils of his eyes. His face was all screwed up with the intensity of watching me and it was all I could do to hold still in the chair. I covered by dragging in another lungful of smoke and letting it go toward the ceiling so I could do something with my mouth except feel it try to stretch out of shape.

The picture was perfect now. It was the most beautiful piece of art work I had ever seen. The only trouble was I couldn't make out what it was all about nor who drew it.

I said, "How much would two million in narcotics before the war be worth now, Pat?"

"About double."

I got up and put on my hat. "That's what you're looking for, friend. A couple of shoe boxes that big. If I find them I'll tell you about it."

"Do *you* know where it is?"

"No. I have a great big fat idea, but if it's stayed buried this long it won't hurt anybody staying buried a while longer. All I want is the person who is after it because that person has Velda. If I have to I'll dig it up and trade for her."

"Where are you going now?"

"I think I'm going out and kill somebody, Pat," I said.

Chapter Eleven

The cop at the switchboard told me to go ahead and use the phone. He plugged in an outside line and I dialed the number that got me Michael Friday. I said, "Your line clear? This is Mike."

"Mike! Yes . . . There's no one here."

"Good. Now listen. There's a place called the Texan Bar on Fifty-sixth Street. Get down there as fast as you can. I'll be waiting. You got that?"

"Yes, but . . ."

I hung up on her. It was the best thing you could do with a woman when you wanted her to move fast. She'd be a good hour getting there which was just what I needed.

They were changing shifts outside the building and the flow of cops was getting thicker. I stepped outside, flagged down a cab and gave him the address of Al Affia's place. The rain had thinned traffic down to a minimum and he didn't take long getting there.

Nothing had changed. The blood was still there on the floor, dried into a crusty maroon. Close to the door the air was a little foul and inside it was worse. I shoved the door open, snapped on the light and there was Al grinning at me from the corner of the room, but it was a horrible kind of grin because somebody had broken him into pieces with the whisky bottle. He wasn't killed plain. He was killed fancy as a person could be killed. He was killed so that he couldn't make any sound as he died and whoever did it must have had a great time laughing because Al died slow.

What I came for was gone. There were still two of the blueprints on the table but they showed the layout of the docks. The rest were missing. I picked the phone up, dialed the operator and said very quietly, "Operator . . . get me the local office of the F.B.I."

Somebody said briskly, "Federal Bureau of Investigation, Moffat speaking."

"You better get down here, Moffat," I said. I laid the phone down gently alongside the base and walked out.

They'd know. They were lads you never noticed in the crowd, but they were all eyes and ears and brains. They worked quietly and you never read about them in the papers, but they got things done and they'd know. Maybe they knew a lot more than I thought they'd know.

She was waiting for me at the bar. She was a lusty, beautiful woman with a mouth that made you hungry when she smiled at you as you came in. There was humor in her eyes, but the wonder and curiosity showed below in the little lines that radiated from the corners of her lips.

There was nothing in mine. I could feel them

flat and dull in their sockets. I nudged my chin to the booths in the back and she followed me. We sat down and she waited for me to say something and all I could think of was the last time I had sat here it was with Velda and now time was getting short.

I took the cigarette she held out from the case, lit it and leaned on the table. "How much do you love your brother, kid?"

"Mike . . ."

"I'm asking the questions."

"He's my brother."

"Partially."

"That doesn't matter."

"He's mixed up in one of the dirtiest rackets you'll ever find. He has a part in it someplace and is paid off in the blood and terror you'll find wherever you find the Mafia operating. He's part of a chain of killers and thieves, yet you like what his money can buy. Your love doesn't stop anyplace, does it?"

She sat away from me as if I held a snake out at her.

"Stop, Mike, please stop!"

"You can stay on his side or mine, kid. The choice is up to you."

The hysteria was caught in her chest. Her mouth wasn't pretty any more. One little sob got loose and that was all. "Al Affia is dead. So far he's the latest. He isn't the last. Where do you stand?"

It came out slowly. She fought it all the way and won it. "With you, Mike."

"I need some information. About Berga Torn."
She dropped her head and toyed with the ashtray.
"Your brother played around with her some time
ago. Why?"

"He . . . hated that woman. She was a tramp.
He hated tramps."

"Did she know it?"

Michael shook her head. "In public he seemed
fond of her. When we were alone . . . he said
awful things about her."

"How far did he go?"

She looked up helplessly. "He kept her. I don't
know why he did it . . . he didn't like her at
all. The woman he did care for at the time left
him because he spent all his time . . . nights
. . . with Berga. Carl . . . was upset about it.
One night he had an argument with someone about
her in his study. He was so mad afterward he went
out and got drunk, but he never saw Berga after
that. He had an argument with her, too."

"You know about Carl's testifying before a congressional committee?"

"Yes. It . . . didn't seem to bother him. Not
until . . . he heard that . . . she was going to
speak against him."

"That was never made public."

"Carl has friends in Washington," she said simply.

"Yet he never worried about it?"

"No."

"Let's go back further, sugar. Let's go back before the war. Was there any time you can remem-

ber when something bothered Carl so much it damn near drove him nuts?"

The shadows around her eyes deepened, her hands pressed together tightly and she said, "How did you know? Yes, there was . . . a time."

"Now go over it slowly. Think about it. What did he do?"

Something panicky crossed her face. "I . . . nothing. He was hardly ever home. He wouldn't let me talk to him at all. When he was at home all he did was make long-distance calls. I remember because the phone bill was almost a thousand dollars for the month."

My breath was coming in hot. It hissed in between my teeth with a whisper and burned into my lungs. I said, "Can you get that bill? Can you get the itemized list that went with it?"

"I . . . might. Carl keeps everything . . . in the safe at home. Once I saw the combination on the back of the desk blotter."

I wrote down an address. Pat's. But all I gave her was the address and the apartment number. "Find it. When you do, bring it here." I folded the paper into her hand and she dropped it into her bag after looking at it long enough to etch it into her memory.

He'd get it. He'd pass it on and the boys in the blue suits would tie into it. They had the men and the time and the means. They'd do in a day what it would take me a year to do.

I snubbed out my butt, pulled the belt tight on the trench coat and stood up. "You'll spend the rest of your life hating yourself for doing this. Hating me too. If it gets too much I'll take you around and show you a lot of dirty little kids who are orphans and some widows your own age. I can show you pictures of bodies so cut up you'll get sick. I'll show you reports of kids who have killed and are condemned to death because they were sky-high on dope when they decided to see what it was like to burn a man down. You won't be stopping it all. You'll slow it down a little, maybe, but a few people who would have died will go on living because of you."

For a few seconds she seemed completely empty. If there was any emotion in her it had drained out and all she was left with were her thoughts. They showed on her face, every one of them. They showed when she looked back into the past and brought to life what she had known all along but had refused to acknowledge. They showed when the life came back to her eyes and her mouth. She tilted one eyebrow at me, did something to her head that shook her hair loose down her back.

"I won't hate you, Mike. Myself, perhaps, but not you."

I think she knew it then. The thought of it hung in the air like a charged cloud. Michael said, "They'll finally kill me, won't they, Mike." It wasn't a question.

"What's left of them . . . if they ever find out . . . would like to think they will. They'd like to kill me too. You can always remember one thing because they'll be remembering it too. They're

208

not as big as they think they are."

She smiled, a wan, drawn smile. "Mike . . ."

I took the hand she held out to me.

"Kiss me again. Just in case."

The wetness glistened on her lips. They were firm lips, large, ripe, parted slightly over the even lines of her teeth. There was fire there that grew hotter as I came closer. I could see her mouth open even more, the tip of her tongue impatiently waiting, then the impatience broke and it met me before lips did.

I held her face in my hands, heard the soft moan she made, felt her nails biting into my arms through the coat, then I let her go. She trembled so violently she had to press her hands against the booth and the fiery liquid of her mouth passed on into her eyes.

"Please go, Mike," she said.

And I went. The rain took me back again, put its arms around me and held tight. I became part of the night, part of the wet, part of the noise and life that was the city. I could hear it laughing at me, a low, dull rumble with a sneer in it.

I walked down the side streets, crossed the avenues and got back to my kind of people again. I drifted through the night while my mind was days away and I was saying it off to myself and wondering how many other people were doing the same things. I was looking at a picture through the rain, knowing what was going on and not being able to make out the details.

It was a picture of a grim organization that

stretched out its tentacles all over the world with the tips reaching into the highest places possible. It was an organization fed on the money of destruction and one tentacle was starving. The two million that was sent to feed it never arrived. No, that was wrong. It did arrive, but someplace it sat and was still there. In its sitting it had doubled its worth and the tentacle wanted it bad. It had to feast now to live. It was after the food with all the fury of its hunger, ready to do anything in the final, convulsive gesture of survival.

You could say it started with Berga. She wasn't the girl in the headlights any longer. She was younger now, a tall luscious Viking with eyes that could draw a man. She was a blonde snare with a body full of playful curves that held out triple challenges, a body full of dares waiting to be taken up. She was coming home from a visit to Italy and in the hidden hours on board that ship she had found a person who was ready to call the dare. He wasn't a special kind of a man. He was a guy with a small export business who could pass unnoticed in the crowd. He was a guy with a legitimate excuse to travel at certain times. He was a guy who was part of a great plan, a guy named Nicholas Raymond who really wasn't anything at all and because of it was the one they used as a messenger to bring in the vital food for the tentacle over here.

But he had a fault and because of it a lot of people died and the tentacle was starving. He liked the women. And Berga was special. He liked her so much he never followed the plan of delivery through and made plans to use the stuff himself. He and Berga. Two million bucks after conversion. Tax free. Someplace the stuff was still there. Maybe it took them a long time to find him again, or maybe they wanted the stuff first and were afraid the secret would die with him. However it was it took him a while to die. Maybe they thought Berga had it then. And she died. That put it on me.

I was thinking of something then. Horror, terror, fear . . . all of it that was there in her face for a little while, a confusion of emotions that stopped too suddenly.

I cursed to myself as the minute details started to fall into place, spun around and yelled at a cab. He jammed on the brakes, swerved slightly and was hardly stopped before I had the door opened. I told him where to take me and sat on the edge of the seat until we got there.

The elevator took me up to my office. I got out jangling my keys from my hand, stuck one in the lock and turned it. The outer office was empty, her typewriter a forlorn thing under its cover. Velda's desk was covered with mail separated into classified piles of bills, personals and miscellaneous. I went through them twice, didn't find what I was looking for, then spotted the pile that had come through the door slot I had pushed aside when I came in. There wasn't anything there, either. I went back to the desk, the curse still in my mouth when I saw it. The sheet lay under the stapler with the top under the flap of the envelope. I turned it over and saw the trade name of a gasoline company.

It was simple statement. One line. *"The way to a man's heart —"* and under it the initials, *"B. T."* Velda would have known, but Velda never saw it. Berga must have scribbled it at the service station after lifting the address from the registration tacked to the steering post of my heap, but it was the old address. The new one was on the back out of sight and she hadn't seen the lines drawn through the words that voided it.

I looked at it, remembered her face again and knew what she was thinking when she wrote it. I felt the thing crumple in my hand as I squashed it in my fingers and never heard the door open behind me.

He stood in the doorway of my inner office and said, "I trust you can make something out of it. We couldn't."

I knew he had a gun without looking. I knew there were more of them without seeing them and I didn't give a damn in the world because I knew the voice. *I knew the voice and it was the one I said I'd never forget!* The last time it spoke I was supposed to die and before it could speak again I let out a crazy sound of hate that filled the room and was at them in a crouch with the bullets spitting over my head. I had the guy in my hands feeling my fingers tear his eyes loose while he screamed his lungs out and even the gun butt pounding on the back of my skull didn't stop me. I had enough left to lash out with my foot and hear it bite into flesh and bone and enough left to do something to one of them that turned his stomach inside out in my face. The horrible, choked scream of anguish one was letting out on the floor diminished to a whimper before disappearing altogether in the blackness that was closing in around me. Far in the distance I thought I heard sharp, flat sounds and a voice swearing hoarsely. Then I heard nothing at all.

It was a room. It had one window high off the floor and you could see the pinpoints that were stars through the film of dirt on the glass. I was spread-eagled on the bed with my hands and legs pulled tight to the frame and when I tried to twist the ropes bit into my skin and burned like acid. The muscles in my side had knotted in pain over ribs that were torturous hands gripping my chest.

There was a taste of blood in my mouth and as I came awake my stomach turned over and dragged long, agonized retches up my throat. I tried to breathe as deeply as I could, draw the air down to stop the retching. It seemed to take a long time before it stopped. I lifted my head and felt my hair stick to the bed. The back of it throbbed and felt like it was coming off so I let it ease back until the giddiness passed.

The room took shape, a square empty thing with a musty odor of disuse filling it. I could see the single chair in one corner, the door in the wall and the foot of the bed. I tried to move, but there wasn't an inch of play in the ropes and the knots that tied them only seemed to get tighter.

I wondered how long I had been there. I listened for sounds I could place but all I got was the steady drip of water outside the window. It was still raining. I listened even more intently, straining my ears into the silence and then I knew about how long I had been there.

My watch had stopped. I could see the luminous hands and number so it hadn't broken . . . it just stopped. This wasn't the same night it had happened. Everything I felt seemed to pour out of my mouth and I fought those damned ropes with every ounce of strength in me. They bit in, cut deeper and held like they were meant to and when I knew it wasn't any use fighting them I slumped back cursing myself for being so jackassed stupid as to walk into the deal without a rod and let them take me. I cursed myself for letting Velda do what she wanted to and cursed myself for not playing it right with Pat. No, I had to be a damned hero. I had to make it by myself. I had to take on the whole organization at once knowing what they were like and how they operated. I passed out advice all around then forgot to give some of it to myself.

There were footsteps in the other room that padded up to the door. It opened into an oblong of yellow light framing the man and the one behind him who stood there. They were opaque forms without faces but it didn't matter any more. One said, "He awake?"

"Yeah, he's out of it."

They came in and stood over me. Two of them

and I could see the billies in their hands.

"Tough guy. You were hard to take, mister. You know what you did? You pulled the eyes right out of Foreman. He screamed so loud my friend here had to tap him one and he tapped too hard and now Foreman's lying in a Jersey swamp dead. They don't come like Foreman any more. You know something else? You ruptured Duke, you bastard. You fixed him good, you did."

"Go to hell," I said.

"Still tough. Sure, you got to keep up the act. You know it won't do any good even if you got down on your knees and begged." He grunted out a laugh. "Pretty soon the boss is coming in here. He's going to ask you some questions and to make sure you answer we're going to soften you up a little bit. Not much . . . just a little bit."

The billy went up slowly. I couldn't keep my eyes off it. The thing reached his shoulder then snapped down with a blur of motion and smashed into my ribs. They both did it then, a pair of sadistic bastards trying to kill me by inches, then one made the mistake of cutting for my neck and got the side of my head instead and that wonderful, sweet darkness came back again where there was no more pain or sound and I tumbled headlong into the pool.

But the same incredible pain that had brought the sleep brought the awakening. It was a pain that turned my whole body into a mass of broken nerve ends that shrieked their messages to my brain. I lay there with my mouth open sucking in air, wishing I could die, but knowing at the same time I couldn't yet.

The body doesn't stand for that kind of torture very long. It shocks itself into forgetting it and soon the pain goes away. It isn't gone for good, but the temporary relief is a kiss of love. It lies there in that state of extreme emergency, caring for its own, and when the realization of another emergency penetrates it readies itself to act again.

I had to think. There had to be a gimmick somewhere and I had to find it. I could see the outlines of the bed and feel the ropes that tied me to the steel frame. It was one of those fold-away things with a heavy innerspring mattress and I was laced down so tightly my hands dented the rolled edges of it. I looked down at my toes, over my head at my hands and took the only way out.

There was noise to it, time involved, and pressures that start the blood flowing down my wrists again. I rocked the bed sideways until it teetered on edge, then held my breath as it tipped. I hit the floor and the thing came halfway over on top of me before it slithered back on its side. The mattress had pulled out from under my feet and when I kicked around I got the lower half entirely free of the springs. I had to stop and get my breath, then when I tried the second time it came away from under my hands too and I had the play in the ropes that I needed. They were wet and slippery with my own blood. My fingernails broke tugging at them, but it was the blood that did it. I felt one come free, the next one and my hand

216

was loose. It only took a few minutes longer to get the other one off and my feet off the end of the bed and I was standing up with my heart trying to pound the shock away and the pain back in place.

I didn't let it get that far. I was half drugged with exertion but I knew what I had to do. I put the bed back on its legs, spread the mattress out and got back the way I had been. I was able to dummy the ropes around both feet and one hand and hoped they wouldn't see the one I couldn't get to.

Time. Now I could use a little time. Every second of it put strength back in my body. I lay there completely relaxed, my eyes closed. I tried to bring the picture back in focus and got part of it. I got Berga and Nicholas Raymond and a guy pushing him into the path of a truck. I was thinking that if they had pulled an autopsy on the body they would have found a jugful of stuff in his veins that made him a walking automaton.

The picture got just a little bit clearer and I could see the work they did on Berga. Oh, it had to be easy. With two million bucks in the bag you don't barge around until you're sure what you're doing. First they tried to scare her, then came the big con job. Carl Evello, the man-about-town putting on the heavy rush act, trying to get close enough to the babe to see what she knew.

I thought about it while I lay there, trying to figure the mind of one little guy who thought he could beat the Mafia out of a fortune and pretty soon I was reading his thoughts as if they were my own. Raymond had planned pretty well. In some way he had planted the secret of his cache with Berga so that she'd have to do some tall thinking to get to it. It had taken her a long time, but she had finally caught on and the Mafia knew when she did. She had hired a bodyguard that didn't work but she still wouldn't let go of what she knew because as soon as she did she'd take the long road too. Maybe she saw her way out of it when Uncle Sam put the squeeze on Evello. Maybe she thought with him away she'd have a chance. If she did she thought wrong. They still got to her.

My eyes opened and squinted at the ceiling. A couple more details were looking for a place to crawl into and I was just about to shove them there when I heard the voices outside.

They didn't try to be quiet. Two of them were bragging that I'd be ready to spill my guts and the other one said I had better be. It was a quiet voice that wasn't a bit new to me. It said, "Wait here and I'll see."

"You want us to come in, boss? He might need more softening."

"I'll call you if he does."

"Okay, boss."

Chairs rasped against the floor as the door opened. I could see the two of them there starting to open a bottle on the table, then the door closed and he was feeling for a light switch. He swore at the blackness, struck a match and held it out in front of him. There was no light, but a candle in a bottle was on the chair and he lit it. He put the bottle down beside me, drew up the chair and lit a cigarette.

The smoke tasted sweet in my nostrils. I licked my lips as I watched the butt glow a deep red and he grinned as he blew the cloud across my face.

I said, "Hello, Carl." I made it good and snotty, but he didn't lose the grin.

"The infamous Mike Hammer. I hope the boys did a good job. They can do a better one if I let them."

"They did a good job."

I rolled my head and took a good look at him. "So you're . . . the boss."

The grin changed shape this time. One side of it dropped caustically. "Not quite . . . yet." The evil in his eyes danced in the candlelight. "Perhaps by tomorrow I will be. I'm only the boss locally . . . now."

"You louse," I said. The words seemed to have an effort to them. My breathing was labored, coming through my teeth. I closed my eyes, stiffened and heard him laugh.

"You did a lot of legwork for us. I hear you blundered right on what we have been looking for."

I didn't say anything.

"You wanted to trade. Where is it?"

I let my eyes come open. "Let her go first."

He gave me that twisted grin again. "I'm not trading for her. Funny enough, I don't even know where she is. You see, she wasn't part of my department."

219

It took everything I could do to hold still. I could feel the nervous tremors creeping up my arms and I made fists of my hands to keep from shaking.

"It's you I'm trading for. You can tell me or I can walk out of here and say something to the boys. You'll want to talk then."

"The hell with you."

He leaned a little closer. "One of the boys is a knife man. He likes to do things with a knife. Maybe you can remember what he did to Berga Torn." I could see the smile on his face get ugly. "That isn't even a little bit what he'll do to you."

The side of his hand traced horrible gestures across my body, meaningful, cutting gestures with the nastiest implications imaginable in them. Then the gestures ended as the side of his palm sliced into my groin for emphasis and the yell that started in my throat choked off in a welter of pain and I mumbled something Carl seemed to want to hear and he bent forward saying, "What? What?"

And that repeated question was the last Carl Evello ever spoke again because he got too close and there were my hands around his throat squeezing so hard his flesh buried my fingers while his eyes were hard little marbles trying to roll out of their sockets. I squeezed and pushed him on his knees and there wasn't even any sound at all. His fingernails bit into my wrists with an insane fury that lived only a few seconds, then relaxed as his head went back with his tongue swelling in the gaping opening that was his mouth. Things in his throat stretched and popped and when I let go there was only the slightest wheeze of air that trickled back into lungs that were almost at the bursting point.

I got him on the bed. I spread him out the way I had been and let him lie there. The joke was too good to pass up so Carl lived a minute longer than he should have. I tried to make my voice as close to his as I could and I called to the door, "He talked. Now put him away."

Outside a chair scraped back. There was a single spoken word, silence, and the slow shuffle of footsteps coming toward the door. He didn't even look at me. He walked up to the bed and I could hear the *snick* as the knife opened. The boy was good. He didn't drive it in. He put it in position and pushed. Carl's body ached, trembled and as I stepped away from the candle the boy saw the mistake and knew he had made his last one. I put everything I could find into the swing that caught the side of his neck and mashed his vertebrae into his spinal cord and he was dead before I eased him to the floor.

Cute. Getting cuter all the time.

I came out of the door with a yell I couldn't keep inside me and dived at the guy at the table. His frenzied stare of hesitation cost him the second he needed to clear his rod and while he was still digging for it my fingers were ripping into his face and my body smashed him right out of the chair. The gun hit the floor and bounced across the room. My knees slammed into him, brought a scream bubbling out of his mouth that snapped off when my fist twisted his jaw out of shape. He didn't try for the gun any more. He just reached for his face and tried to cover it but I didn't let him have the pleasure out of not seeing what was happening. His eyes had to watch everything I did to him until they filmed over and blanked out when the back of his head cracked against the floor. The blood trickled out his nose and ears when I stood over him, a bright red that seemed to match the fire burning in my lungs. I pulled him inside to the other two, tangled his arms around the boy who still held the knife and left them that way.

Then I left. I got out on the street and let the rain wash me clean. I breathed the air until the fire went out, until some of the life I had left back inside crawled into my system again.

The guy sitting in the doorway ten feet away heard me laugh. His head jerked up out of the drunken stupor and he looked at me. Maybe he could see the way my face was and understand what was behind the laugh. The eyes bleary with cheap whisky lost their glassiness and he trembled a little bit, trying to draw back into his doorway. My laugh got louder and he couldn't stand it, so he stood up and lurched away, looking back twice to make sure I was still there.

I knew where I was. Once you put in time on Second Avenue you never forget it. The store front I came out of was dirty and deserted. At one time it had been a lunch counter, but now all that was left was the grease stains and the *FOR RENT* sign in the window. The gin mill on the corner was

222

just closing up, the last of the human rubble that inhabited the place drifting across the street until he dissolved into the mist.

I walked slow and easy, another one of the dozens you could see sprawled out away from the rain. Another joe looking for a place to park, another joe who couldn't find one. I made the police call box on the second corner down, got it open and said hello when I heard the voice answer. I didn't have to try hard to put a rasp into my voice. I said, "Copper, you better get somebody down this way fast. Somebody screaming his head off in that empty dog wagon two blocks south."

Two minutes were all they took. The siren whined through the rain and the squad car passed me with its tires spitting spray. They'd find a nice little mess, all right. The one guy left could talk his head off, but he was still going to cook in the hot squat up the river.

I pulled my wallet out and went through it. Everything was there except money. Even my change was gone. I needed a dime like I never needed one before and there wasn't even a character around to bum one from. Down the street lights of a diner threw a yellow blob on the sidewalks. I walked toward it, stood outside the door a second looking at the two drunks and the guy with the trombone case perched on the stools.

There wasn't any more I could lose so I walked in, called the counterman over and tossed my watch on the counter. "I need a dime. You can hold my watch."

"For a dime? Mac, you nuts? Look, if you need some coffee say so."

"I don't need coffee. I want to make a phone call."

His eyes went up and down me and his mouth rounded into a silent "oh." "You been rolled, huh?" He fished in his pocket, tossed a dime on the counter and pushed my watch back to me. "Go ahead, mac, I know how it is."

Pat wasn't at home. My dime clinked back and I tried his office. I asked for Captain Chambers and he wasn't there either. The cop on the board wanted to take a message and the captain would take care of it when he came in. I said, "Pal, this kind of message won't wait. It's something he's been working on and if I can't get word to him right away he's going to hit the roof."

The phone dimmed out as the operator spoke away from it. I could hear the hurried exchange of murmurs, then: "We'll try to contact the captain by radio. Can you leave your phone number?"

I read it off the dial, told him I'd wait and hung up. The counterman was still watching me. There was a steaming hot cup of coffee by an empty stool with a half pack of butts lying alongside it. The guy grinned, nodded to the coffee and made himself a friend. Coffee was about all my stomach would hold, but it sat there inside me like a million bucks in my hand. It took the shakes out of my legs and the ache from my body.

I lit a smoke, relaxed and watched the window. The wind in the street whipped the rain against the plate glass until it rattled. The door opened, a damp blast momentarily freshening the air. Another musician with a fiddle case under his coat sat down tiredly and ordered coffee. Someplace off in the distance a siren moaned, and a minute later another crossed its fading echo. Two more came on top of it, not close, but distant voices racing to a sore spot in the great sprawling sick body of the city.

Corpuscles, I thought. That's what they were like. White corpuscles getting to the site of the infection. They'd close in and wipe out the parasites and if they were too late they'd call for the carpenter corpuscles to come and rebuild broken tissue around the wound.

I was thinking about it when Pat walked in, tired lines around his eyes, his face set in a frozen expression. There was a twitch in the corner of his mouth he tried to wipe away with the back of his hand.

He came over and sat down. "Who kicked the crap out of you, Mike?"

"I look that bad?"

"You're a mess."

I could grin then. Tomorrow, the next day, the day after, maybe, I'd be too sore to move, but right then I could grin. "They reached me but they didn't hold on to me, chum."

His eyes got narrow and very, very bright. "There was a dirty little mess not too far from here. That wouldn't be it, would it?"

"How good is it like it stands?"

225

Pat's lips came apart over his teeth. "The one guy left is wanted for three different kills. This one finishes him."

"The coroner say that?"

"Yeah, the coroner says that. I say that. We have two experts on the spot who say that too but the guy doesn't say that. The guy doesn't know what to say. He's still half out and he says things about a girl named Berga Torn he worked over and when he knew what he did it woke him up and now he won't say anything. He's the scaredest clam you ever saw in your life."

"So it stands?"

"Nobody'll break it. Now what do you say about it?" I took a big pull on the butt and stamped it out in the ash tray. "It's a detail. Right now it doesn't mean a damn one way or the other to you or me. Someday over a beer I'll make it into a good story."

"It better be good," Pat said. "I have all hell breaking loose around my ears. Evello's sister came to us with a list of phone calls yesterday and we tracked down the names into the damnedest places you ever saw. We have some of the wheels in the Mafia dangling by their you-know-whats and they're scramming for cover. They're going nuts down in Florida and on the Coast the police have pulled in people big enough to make your hair stand on end. Some of 'em are talking and the thing's opening wider."

He passed his hand over his eyes and drew it away slowly. "Damn it, we're up as far as Washington itself. It makes me sick."

The shake was back in my legs again. "Talk names, Pat."

"Names you don't know and some you do. We have the connections down pat but the ones up top are sitting tight. The Miami police pulled a quick raid on a local big shot and turned up a filing case of information that gives us a line into half the narcotics outlets in the States. Right now the Federal boys have assigned extra men to pick up the stuff and they're coming home loaded."

"How about Billy Mist?" I asked him.

"Nothing doing. Not a word on him so far. He can't be located, anyway."

"Leo Harmody?"

"You got another case? He's howling police persecution and threatening to take things up with Congress. He can yell because there's nothing we can slap him with."

"And Al Affia's dead," I said.

Pat's head turned toward me, his eyes a sleepy gray. "You wouldn't know anything about that, would you?"

"It couldn't've happened to a better guy."

"He was chopped up good. Somebody had a little fun."

I looked at him, lit another smoke and flipped the match in the ash tray where it turned into a charred arc. "How far did you get with him?"

"Not a thing. There wasn't a recognizable print on that bottle."

"What's the word on it, Pat?"

His eyes got sleepier. "His waterfront racket is going sky-high. There's been two killings down there already. The king is dead, but somebody is ready to take his place."

The rain had the sound of a rolling snare drum. It was working up in tempo, backed by the duller, more resonant peals of thunder that cracked the sky open. The three drunks stared at the window miserably, hugging their cups as an anchor to keep from drifting out into the night. The fiddle player shrugged, paid his bill and tucked the case back under his coat and left. At least he was lucky enough to grab an empty cab going by.

I said, "Do you have the picture yet, Pat?"

"Yeah, I have a picture," he said. "It's the biggest one I ever saw."

"You're lost, kid."

The sleepiness left his eyes. His fingers turned the ash tray around slowly, then he gave me that wry grin of his. "Play it out, Mike."

I shrugged. "Everything's coming your way. Now you're having fun. What started it?"

"Okay, so it began with Berga."

"Let's not forget it. Let's tie it all up together so when you're out there having fun you'll know why. I'll make it short and sweet and you can check on it. Ten, twelve, maybe fifteen years ago a guy was bringing a package of dope into the country for delivery to the Mafia. He tangled with a dame on board and fell for her. That's where Berga came into it. Instead of handing over the package he decided to keep it for his sweetie and himself even though he ran the risk of being knocked off."

"Nicholas Raymond," Pat said.

I knew the surprise showed on my face when I nodded. "Nicholas had them on the spot. They couldn't bump him until they located the stuff and he wasn't stupid enough to lead them to it. There was two million bucks' worth in that consignment and they needed it badly. So Nick goes on living with this gal and one day he dies accidentally. It's a tricky pitch but it isn't a hard one. They figured that by this time he would have passed the secret along to her or she would have found out herself somehow.

"But it didn't happen that way. Nick was trickier than they thought. He got the word to her in case something happened to him but, even she didn't know where it was or what it was that keyed it. I guess they must have tried to scare it out of her for a while because she hired herself a bodyguard. He played it too good and moved in. The Mafia didn't like that. If he came across the stuff they'd be out of luck, so he went too."

Pat was watching me closely. There was an expression on his face like I wasn't telling him anything new, but he wasn't saying a word.

"Now we come to Evello. He gets a proper knockdown to her somehow and off he goes on the big pitch. He gave her the whole treatment and probably winds it up with a proposal of marriage to make it sound good. Maybe he over-played his hand. Maybe he just wasn't smart enough to fool her. Something slipped and Berga got wise that he was one of the mob. But she got wise to something else too. *About then she suddenly discovered what it was they were all after and when she had the chance to get Evello creamed before that congressional committee she put in her bid figuring to get the stuff on her own hook later.*"

Now Pat's face was showing that he didn't know it all. There were sharp lines streaking out from the corners of his eyes and he waited, his tongue wetting down his lips from time to time.

I said, "She pulled out all the stops and so did they. The boys with the black hands get around. They scared her silly and by that time it didn't take much. She went to pieces and tried to fight it out in that sanitarium."

"That was her biggest mistake," Pat said.

"You mentioned a woman who came to see her."

He gave a slow nod, his hands opening and closing slowly. "We still can't make her."

"Could it have been a man dressed like a dame?"

"It could have been anything. There was no accurate description and no record of it."

"It was somebody she knew."

"Great."

"Now the stuff is still missing."

"I know where it is."

Pat's head came around faster this time.

"The two million turned into four by just sitting there," I said. "Inflation."

"Damn it, Mike, where?" His voice was all tight.

"On the good ship *Cedric*. Our friend Al Affia

230

was working on the deal. He had given all the plans to her in his dive back there and whoever killed him walked off with them."

"Now you tell me," he said hoarsely. "Now you spill it when somebody has had time to dig it loose."

I took a deep breath, grunted when the sting of pain stabbed across my chest and shook my head. "It's not that easy, Pat. Al had those plans a long time. I'm even beginning to think I know why he was bumped."

Pat waited me out.

"He tried to sucker Velda into his dump for a fast play at her. She slipped him a dose of chloral and while he was out started turning the place upside down. Al didn't stay out very long. He got sick, his stomach dumped the stuff overboard and he saw what she was doing. Velda used the bottle on him then."

His eyes snapped wide open. "Velda!"

"She didn't kill him. She bopped him one and it cut his head open. He staggered out after her and got word to somebody. That somebody caught the deal in a hurry and someplace she's still sweating." All at once every bit of pain in my body flooded back and trapped me in its agony before fading away. I finished with, "I hope."

"Okay, Mike, let it loose! Damn it, what else have you got? So the kid's sweating, you hope . . . and I hope too. You know them well enough to realize what's liable to happen to her now."

"She was on her way to see Billy Mist." My

grin turned sour and my teeth came out from under my lips again. "The cops didn't find her."

"Supposing she never reached there?"

"It's a possibility I've been considering, friend. I saw her pass in a cab and she wasn't alone."

I was going warm again. The coffee didn't sit so well in my gut any more. I thought about it as long as I could then shut out the picture when I buried my face in my hands.

Pat kept saying, "The bastards, the bastards!" His nails made a tattoo of sound on the counter and his breathing was almost as hard as mine was. "It's breaking fast, but it's not wide open yet, Mike. We'll get to Billy. One way or another."

I felt a little better. I took my hands away and reached for the last butt in the pack. "It won't break until you get the stuff. You and the whole staff up in Washington can work from now until ten years later and you won't make a hole in the organization big enough to stop it. You'll knock it kicking but you won't kill it. Slowing it down a little is all we can hope for. They're going to hang on to Velda until somebody has that four million bucks lined up.

"I'm the target, chum. Me personally. I've scared the crap out of those guys as individuals . . . not as an organization. They know I don't give a damn what happens to the outfit, the dough or anything that goes with it. All I want is a raft of hides nailed to the barn door. That's where I come in. I'm the little guy with a grudge. I'm the guy so damn burned up he's after a man, not

232

an organization. I'm the guy who wants to stand there and see him die and he knows it. He wants that consignment of narcotics in the worst way but before it does him any good I have to die first.

"So they're holding Velda. She's the bait and she's something else besides. I've been getting closer to this than anybody else and they've known something I never got wise to. Berga passed the clue to me before she died and I've been sitting on it all this time. For a little while they had it, but they couldn't make it out. They expect me to. When I do I'll have to use it to ransom Velda with it."

"They're not that dumb, Mike," Pat told me.

"Neither am I. Someplace the answer slapped me in the teeth and I was in such a hurry I missed it. I can feel the damn thing crawling around in my head and can't lay my finger on it. The damn arrogant bastards . . ."

Pat said, "The head is pretty far from the body."

"What?"

He looked out the window and watched the rain. "They can afford to be arrogant. The entire structure of the Mafia is built on arrogance. They flaunt the laws of every country in the world, they violate the integrity of the individual, they're a power in themselves backed by ruthlessness, violence and some of the shrewdest brains in existence."

"About the head and the body, I mean."

"We can smash the body of this thing, Mike, but in this country the head and the body aren't connected except by the very thin thread of a neck.

The top man, men, or group is a separate caste. The organization is built so that the head can function without the body if it comes to it. The body parts can be assembled any time, but it's an assembly for the benefit of the head, never forget that. It's a government. The little people in it don't count. Its the rulers who are important and the government is run solely for their benefit and to satisfy their appetites. They're never known and they're not going to be known."

"Unless they make one stinking little mistake," I said.

Pat stopped looking at the rain.

I rubbed the ache out of my side. "The stuff is on the *Cedric*. All you have to do is find the ship. The records will carry the stateroom Raymond used. When you find it call Ray Diker at the *Globe* and give him first crack at the details of the yarn. Tell him to hold the story until I call you. By then I'll have Velda."

"Where are you going?"

"The last time you asked that I said I was going out to kill somebody." I held out my hand. "Gimmie a fin."

He looked puzzled, scowled, then pulled five ones out of his pocket. I laid two of them on the counter and nodded to the counterman to come get it. He was all smiles.

"Where's Michael Friday?"

"She said she was going to your place to see you."

"I wasn't home."

"Well, she's not reporting to me on the hour."

"No police guard?"

His frown got bigger this time. "I tried to but she said no. One of the feds pulled out after her anyway. He lost her when she got in a cab."

"Sloppy."

"Lay off. Everybody's up to their ears in this thing."

"Yeah. You going to trace the *Cedric*?"

"What do you think. Where are you going?"

I let a laugh out that sounded hollow as hell. "I'm going out in the rain and think some more. Then maybe I'll go kill somebody else."

I could see Pat remembering the other years. Younger years when the dirt seemed to be only on the surface. When being a cop looked good and the law was for protection and guidance. When there weren't so many strings and sticky red tape and corruption in high places.

His hand went into his pocket and brought out the blued .38. He handed it to me under the shelf of the hanger. "Here, use this for a change."

And I remembered what Velda had said and I shook my head. "Some other time. I like it better this way."

I went out and walked down the street and let the rain hit me in the face. Someplace there was a gimmick and that was what I had to find. I reached the subway kiosk, bought a pack of Luckies and dropped them in my pocket. I waited for the uptown local and got aboard when it came in.

With every jolt the train took I could feel the

shock wear off a little bit more. It got worse and when it was too bad I stood up and leaned against the door watching the walls of the tunnel go by in a dirty blur.

A gimmick. One lousy little gimmick and I could have it. It was there trying to come out and whenever I thought I had it my stomach would retch and I'd lose it.

The train pulled into the station, opened its multitude of mouths but I was the only one who stepped out. I had the platform all to myself then, so I let go and the coffee came up.

There weren't any cabs outside. I didn't waste time waiting for one. I walked toward my apartment not conscious of the rain any more, hardly conscious of the protest my body was setting up. I felt my legs starting to go when I reached the door and the super and his wife took a startled look at me and helped me inside.

Lily Carver came up out of the chair holding back the sharp intake of her breath with the back of her hand. Her eyes went soft, reflected the hurt mine were showing, then she had my hand and helped me into the bedroom.

I flopped on the bed and closed my eyes. Hands loosened my collar and pulled at my shoes. I could hear the super telling his wife to stay out, and hear her frightened sobs. I could hear Lily and feel her hands on my forehead. For a second I glimpsed the white halo of her hair and saw the sensuous curves of her body in hazy detail hovering over me.

The super said, "You want me to call a doctor, Mr. Hammer?"

I shook my head.

"I'll call a cop. Maybe . . ."

I shook my head again. "I'll be okay."

"You feel good enough to talk a minute?"

"What?" I could feel the sleep closing in as I said it.

"A woman was here. Friday, her name was. She left you a note in an envelope and said it was pretty important. She wanted you to see it as soon as yon came in."

"What was in it?"

"I didn't look. Should I open it?"

"Go ahead."

The bed jounced as he got up. It left me rocking gently, a soothing motion of pure comfort and there was a heaviness under my closed eyes too great to fight. Then the bed jounced again as he sat down and I heard the tearing of paper.

"Here it is." His voice paused. "Not much in it though."

"Read it," I said.

"Sure. *'Dear Mike . . . I found the list. Your friend has it. I found something much more important too and must see you at once. Call me. Please call me at once. Love Michael.'* That's all there is to it, Mr. Hammer."

"Thanks," I said, "thanks a lot."

From the other room his wife set up a nervous twittering. His fingers touched me. "Think it'll be all right if I go back?"

Before I could nod Lily said, "Go ahead. I'll take care of him. Thank you so much for everything."

"Well . . . if you need me, just call down."

"I'll do that."

I got my eyes open one last time. I saw the smooth beauty of her face unmarred by anything now. She was smiling, her hands doing things to my clothes. The strange softness was back in her eyes and she whispered, "Darling, darling . . ."

The sleep came. There was a face in it. The face had a rich, wet mouth, full and soft. It kept coming closer, opening slowly. It was Michael and in my dream I grinned at her, fascinated by her lips.

Chapter Twelve

You hurt too much to sleep. You wake up and it hurts more so you try to go back to sleep. There's a physical ache, a gnawing your body tries vainly to beat down and might have if the pain in your mind wasn't even worse. Processions of thoughts hammer at you, gouge and scrape until the brain is a wild thing seeking some kind of release. But there isn't any release. There's fire all around you, the tongues of it licking closer, needling the skin. The brain screams for you to awaken, but if you do you know the other things . . . the thoughts, will be a more searing pain so you fight and fight until the mind conquers and you feel the awakening coming on.

I thought I heard voices and one was Velda's. She kept calling to me and I couldn't answer back. Somebody was hurting her and I mouthed silent curses while I fought invisible bonds that held me tied to the ground. She was screaming, her voice tortured, screaming for me and I couldn't help her. I strained and kicked and fought but the ropes held until I was breathless and I had to lie there and listen to her die.

I opened my eyes and looked into the darkness, knowing it was only a dream but going nuts because I knew it could be real. My breathing was harsh, laboring, drying my mouth into leathery tissue.

The covers were pulled up to my neck, but under them there was nothing. The skin over my bruised muscles felt cool and pliable, then I found the answer with the tips of my fingers as they slid along flesh that had been gently oiled with some aromatic unguent. From somewhere the faint clean odor of rubbing alcohol crossed my nostrils, disturbing because of its unusual pungent purity. It was the raw smell of fine chemistry, the sharp, natural smell you might expect, but don't find in fresh, virgin forests.

Slowly, waiting for the ache to begin, I pulled my arm free, laid it across the bed, felt the warmth of a body under the back of my hand, then jerked it away as she almost screamed and pulled out of reach to sit there bolt upright with eyes still dumb with sleep reflecting some emotion nobody in the world would be able to put his finger on.

"Easy, Lily . . . It's only me."

She let her breath out with more of a gasp than a sigh, trying to wipe the sleep from her eyes. "You . . . scared me, Mike. I'm sorry." She smiled, sat on the edge of the bed and put her shoes on.

Her dreams must have been pretty rough too. She had taken care of me, lay there while I slept until her eyes closed too. She was a good kid who had been through the mill and was scared to death of a return trip. She wasn't going to get it from me.

I said, "What time is it?"

Lily checked her watch. "A little after nine. Can I get you something to eat?"

"What happened to the day?"

"You slept through. You groaned and talked . . . I didn't want to wake you up, Mike. Can I get you some coffee?"

"I can eat. I need something in my gut."

"All right. I'll call you." Her mouth creased in a smile, one corner of it pulling up with an odd motion. I let my eyes drift over her slowly. As they moved her hands tightened at her throat and the strangeness came back in her face. The smile disappeared into a tight grimace and she twisted around to go out the door.

Some of them are funny, I thought. Beautiful kids who would do anything one minute and scared stiff of doing it the next.

I heard her in the kitchen, got up, showered, managed to get the brush off my face and climbed into some clean clothes. I could hear things frying when I got on the phone and dialed Michael Friday's number.

The voice that answered was deep and guarded. It said, "Mr. Evello's residence," but the touch of Brooklyn in the tone was as plain as the badge it wore.

"Mike Hammer. I'm looking for Michael Friday, Carl's sister. She there?"

"I'm afraid . . ."

"Is Captain Chambers there?"

241

It caught the voice off base a second. "Who'd you say this was?"

"Hammer. Mike Hammer."

There was a muffled consultation, then: "This is the police, Hammer, what did you want?"

"I told you. I want Friday."

"So do we. She isn't around."

"Damn!" It exploded out of me. "You staked out there?"

"That's right. We're covering the place. You know where the girl is?"

"All I know is that she wants to see me bad, feller. How can I reach Chambers?"

"Wait a minute." The phone blanked out again and there was more talk behind a palm stretched over the mouthpiece. "You gonna be where you are a while?"

"I'll be here."

"Okay, the sergeant here says he'll try to get him for you. What's your number?"

"He knows it. Tell him to call me at home."

"Yeah. You get anything on that Friday dame, you pass it this way."

"No leads?"

"No nothing. She disappeared. She came back here after she left headquarters the other day, stayed a couple of hours and grabbed a cab into Manhattan."

"She was coming to see me," I said.

"She was what!"

"I was out. She left a note and took off again. That's why I called her place."

"I'll be damned. We checked all over the city to find out where she went to."

"If she's using cabs maybe you can pick her up from when she left here."

"Sure, sure. I'll pass it along."

The phone went dead and I socked it back in its hanger. Lily called me from the kitchen and I went out and sat down. She had it ready on the table, that same spread like she thought I was two more guys and instead of it looking good my stomach tried to sour at the sight of it. All I could think of was another one gone. Another kid cut down by a pack of scrimy hoods who wanted that two million bucks' worth of hell so bad they'd kill and kill and kill until they had every bit of it.

I smashed my fist into the table saying the same dirty words over and over until Lily's face went a pasty white and she backed against the wall. I was staring into space, but she was occupying the space ahead of me and whatever she saw going across my face made her shrink back even further.

How stupid were they? How far did they have to go? Wasn't their organization big enough to know every damn detail inside and out? They wouldn't be reaching the stuff now, not with the cops going over every inch of the *Cedric*. The whole shebang was coming apart at the edges and instead of piling up the counts against them they ought to be on the run.

Lily slid out of sight. She came up against me and reached out her hand until it was on my shoulder. "Mike . . ."

243

I looked at her without seeing her.

"What is it, Mike?"

The words started out of me. They came slow at first, then turned into a boiling current that was taking in the whole picture. I was almost finished with it when I could feel the sharp points of the gimmicks sticking out and ran my mind back to pick them up. Then I sat and cursed myself because I wasn't fast enough. They weren't there anymore.

There was just one minor little detail. Just a little one I should have thought of long ago. I said to Lily, "Did you go to see Berga Torn in the sanitarium at all?"

Her eyebrows knit, puzzled. "No, I didn't." She pinched her lower lip between her teeth. "I called her twice and the second time she mentioned that someone had been to see her."

I was half out of my chair. "Who? Did she say who?"

She tried hard for it, reaching back through the days. "I think she did. I honestly didn't pay any attention at the time. I was so worried about what was happening it didn't register."

I had her by the shoulders, squeezing my fingers into her skin. "The name's important, kid. That somebody tipped the whole thing. Right then was the beginning of murder that hasn't ended yet. As long as you got that name in your head a killer is going to be prowling around loose and if he ever knows you might have it you're going the same way Berga did."

"Mike!"

244

"Don't worry about it. I'm not letting you out of my sight for a minute any more. Damn it, you got to dig that name out. You understand that?"

"I . . . think I do. Mike, please . . . you're hurting me."

I took my hands down and she rubbed the places where they had bitten in. There were tears in the corners of her eyes, little drops of crystal that swelled and I took a step closer to her. I reached out again, more gently this time, close enough for a second to taste the faint crispness of rubbing alcohol.

Lily smiled again. It was like the first time. The kind of smile you see on the face of a person waiting for death and ready to receive him almost gratefully. "Please eat something, Mike," she whispered.

"I can't, kid. Not now."

"You have to have something in your stomach."

Her words sent something racing up my back. It was a feeling you get when you know you have something and you can't wait to get it out of you. You stand there and wait for the final answer, waiting, waiting, waiting.

It was there in my hand when the phone set up a jangling that wouldn't stop. I grabbed the extension and Pat barked a short hello. I asked him, "Did you find Friday?"

He held his voice down. He sat on it all the way but the roughness showed through anyway. "We didn't find a damn thing. Nothing, got that? No Friday, no jug of hop, no nothing. This town's a madhouse. The feds are cutting a swath through the racket a mile wide and we still haven't come up with the stuff. Mike, if that stuff sits there . . ."

"I know what it means."

"Okay then, are you holding anything back?"

"You know better."

"Then what about Friday? If she was up there . . ."

"She wanted to see me. That's all I know."

"You know what I think?"

"I know what you think," I repeated softly. "Billy Mist . . . where's he?"

"You'd never guess."

"Tell me."

"Right now he's having supper at the Terrace. He's got an alibi for everything we can throw at him and nobody's going to break it for a damn long while. He's got people in Washington batting for him and boys with influence pulling strings so hard they're knocking us silly . . . Mike . . ."

"Yeah?"

"Find Velda?"

"Not yet, Pat. Soon."

"You're not saying it right, friend."

"I know."

"In case it makes you feel better, I put men on it."

"Thanks."

"Figured it might not be holing out like you expected."

"Yeah."

"Something else you better know. Your joint's

been covered. Three guys were stationed around waiting for you. The feds picked them up. One of the muscle lads is in the morgue."

"So?"

"There may be more. Keep your eyes open. You may have a tail or two if you leave. At least one'll be our man."

"They're sticking close to me." I said the words through my teeth.

"You're primed for the kill, Mike. You know why? I'll tell you. News has it you were part of the thing from the beginning. You've been fooling me and everybody else, but they got the pitch. Tell me one thing . . . *have* you been shoving it in me?"

"No."

"Good enough. We'll keep playing it this way then."

"What about the *Cedric*?"

He cursed under his breath. "It's screwballed, Mike. It's the whole, lousy, stinking reason behind all this. The ship is in a Jersey port right now undergoing repairs. She was a small liner before the war and was revamped to carry troops. All the staterooms were torn out of her and junked to make it over into a transport. The stuff might have been there once, but it's been gone a long time now. None of this should've happened at all."

I let a few seconds pass before I spoke. I was feeling cold and dead all over. "You got a lot of people you've been wanting to get."

"Yeah, a lot of them." His voice was caustic.

"A lot of punks. A lot of middle-sized boys. A few big ones. Medusa even lost a few of her heads." He laughed sarcastically. "But Medusa is still alive, buddy. She's one big head who doesn't care how many of her little heads she loses. We can chop all the little ones off and in a few months or years she'll grow a whole new crop as vicious as ever. Yeah, we're doing fine. I thought we did good when I had a look at the shiv hole in Carl. I felt great when I saw Affia's face. They were nothing, Mike. You know how I feel now?"

I didn't answer him. I put the phone back while he was still talking. I was thinking of Michael Friday's wet, wet mouth and the way Al Affia *had* looked and what Carl Evello had told me. I was thinking of undercurrents that could even work through an organization like the Mafia and I knew why Michael Friday had tried to see me.

Lily was a drawn figure slumped in the chair. Her fingers kept pushing the silken strands away from her eyes while she watched me. I said, "Get your coat."

"They'll be waiting for us outside?"

"That's right, they'll be waiting."

Even the last shred of hope she had nursed so long left her face. There was a dullness in her eyes and in the way she walked.

"We'll let them wait," I said, and she turned around and grinned with some of the life back in her.

While I waited for her I turned out the light and stood in front of the window watching the city. The monster squirmed, its bright-colored lights marking the threshing of its limbs, a sprawling octopus whose mouth was hidden under a horribly carved beak. The mouth was open, the beak ready to rip and tear anything that stood in its way. It made sounds out there, incomprehensible sounds that were the muted whinings of deadly terror. There were no spoken words, but the sounds were enough. The meaning was clear.

"I'm ready, Mike."

She had on the green suit again, trimly beautiful, her hair gone now under a pert little hat with a feather in it. The expression on her face said that if she must die it would be quick and clean. And dressed. She was ready. We both were ready. Two very marked people stepping out to look for the mouth of the octopus.

We didn't go down the stairs. We went up to the roof and crossed the abutments between the apartments. We found the door we wanted through the roof of a building a hundred yards down and used that. We took the elevator to the basement and went out through the back. The yard there was an empty place, too steeped in darkness to reflect any of the window lights above. The wall was head-high brick, easy to get over. I pushed Lily up, got over myself and helped her down. We felt our way around the wall until we reached the other basement door but the luck we had had bent a little around a lock under the knob.

I was ready to start working on it when I heard the muffled talk inside and the luck unbent a little bit. I whispered to Lily to keep quiet and pushed her against the side of the building. The talk got louder, the lock clicked and somebody shoved the door open.

The stream of light that flooded the yard didn't catch us. We stayed behind the door and waited. The kid with the wispy mustache backed out swearing under his breath while he tugged at a leash and for a second I was ready to jump him before the racket started. Lily saw it too and grabbed my hand so hard her nails punched holes into my skin. Then the kid was out and walking toward the wall in back with so much to say about people who have cats taken for a walk on a leash that he never saw us go through the door at all.

We got out the other end of the building and circled around the block to the garage. Sammy was just coming on duty and waved my way when he saw us. It was a funny kind of a wave with a motion of the other hand under it. I pushed Lily in ahead of me and closed the door.

Sammy didn't know whether to laugh or not. He decided not to, wrinkled up his face in a serious expression and said, "You hot, Mike?"

"In a way I'm boiling. Why?"

"People been around asking about your new heap. One of the boys tipped me that there's eyes watching for it."

"I heard the story."

"Hear what happened to Bob Gellie?" His face grew pretty serious.

"No."

"He got worked over. Something to do with you."

"Bad?"

"He's in the hospital. Whatever it was he wouldn't talk."

The bastards knew everything. What they didn't know they could find out and when they did the blood ran. The organization. The syndicate. The Mafia. It was filthy, rotten right through but the iron glove it wore was so heavy and so sharp it could work with incredible, terrible efficiency. You worked as they'd tell you to work or draw the penalty. There was no in-between. There was only one penalty. It could be slow or fast, but the result was the same. You died. Until they died, until every damn one of them was nothing but decaying flesh in a pile on the ground the killings would go on and on.

"I'll take care of him. You tell him that for me. How is he?"

"Bob'll come through it. He won't ever look the same, but he'll be okay."

"How do you feel, Sammy?"

"Lousy, if you gotta know. I got me a .32 in the drawer there that's gonna stay right handy all night and maybe afterward."

"Can you get me a car?"

"Take mine. I figured you'd be asking so I have it by the door nosing out. It's a good load and I like it, so bring it back in one piece."

He waved to the door, pulled down the blind over the window and followed us into the garage.

251

He hauled the door up, grinned unhappily when we pulled out and let it slam back in place. I told Lily to get down until I was sure we were clear, made a few turns around one-way streets, parked for a few minutes watching for lights, then pulled out again and cut into traffic.

Lily said, "Where are we going, Mike?"

"You'll see."

"Mike . . . please. I'm awfully scared."

Her lower lip matched the flutter of her voice. She sat there pinching her hands together, her arms making jerky movements against her sides to control the shudder that was trying to take over her body.

"Sorry, kid," I told her. "You're as much a part of this as I am. You ought to know about it. We're going to see what made a woman want to see me pretty badly. We're going to find out what she knew that put her on the missing list. There isn't much you can do except sit tight, but while you're sitting there's plenty you can do. Remember that name. Dig up every detail of that talk you had with Berga and bring that name out."

She looked straight ahead, her face set, and nodded. "All right, Mike. I'll . . . try." Then her head came around and I could feel the challenge of her stare but couldn't match it while I was weaving through the traffic. "I'd do *anything* for you, Mike," she finished softly. There was a newness in her voice I'd never heard before. A controlled excitement that made me remember how I had awakened and what she was thinking of. Before

I could answer she turned her head with the same suddenness and stared straight ahead again, but this time with an excited expression of anticipation.

There were only two men assigned to the place when we got there. One sat in the car and the other was parked in a chair by the door looking like he wanted a cigarette pretty bad. He gave me that frozen look all cops keep in reserve and waited for me to speak my piece.

"I'm Mike Hammer. I've been cooperating with Captain Chambers on the deal here and would like to take a look around. Who do I see?"

The freeze melted loose and he nodded. "The boys were talking about you before. The captain say it's okay?"

"Not yet. He will if you want to go get a call in to him."

"Ah, guess it's okay. Don't touch anything, that's all."

"Anybody around inside?"

"Nope. Joint's empty. The butler took an inventory of liquor before he left though."

"Careful guy. I'll be right out."

"Take your time."

So I went in and stood in the long hallway. I held a light up to the Lucky between my lips and blew a thin overcast into the air. There were lights on along the walls, dim things that gave the place the atmosphere of a funeral parlor and hardly any light.

In the back of my mind I had an idea but I

didn't know how to start it going. You don't walk in and pick up important things after the cops have been through a place. Not unless they don't want what you're looking for.

I made the rounds of the rooms downstairs, finished the butt and snubbed it, then tried upstairs. The layout was equally as elaborate, as well appointed as the other rooms, a chain of bedrooms, a study, a small music room and a miniature hobby shop on the south side. There was one room that smelled of life and living. It had that woman smell I couldn't miss. It had the jaunty, carefree quality that was Michael Friday and when I snapped the lights on I saw I was right.

There was an orderly disarray of things scattered around that said the woman who belonged to the room would be back. The creams, the perfumes, the open box of pins on the dresser. The bed was large with a fluffy-haired poodle doll propped against the pillows. There were pictures of men on the dresser and a couple of enlarged snapshots of Michael in a sailboat with a batch of college boys in attendance.

Scattered, but neat.

Other signs too, professional signs. A cigar ash in the tray. Indentations in the rolled stockings in the box where a thumb had squeezed them. I sat on the edge of the bed and smoked another cigarette. When I had it halfway down I reached over to the night table for an ash tray and laid it on the cover beside me. The tray made an oval in the center of the square there, a boxy outline in dust. I picked it up, looked at the smudge on the cover and wiped at it with my fingertip.

The other details were there too, the thin line of grit and tiny edges of brownish paper that marked the lip of a box somebody had spilled out in emptying it on the bed. With my fingers held together the flat of my hand filled the width of the square and two hands made the length. I finished the butt, put it out and went back downstairs.

The cop on the porch said, "Make out?"

"Nothing special. You find any safes around?"

"Three of 'em. One upstairs, two downstairs. Nothing there we could use. Maybe a few hundred in bills. Take a look yourself. There's a pair in his study."

They were a pair, all right. One was built into the wall behind a framed old map of New York harbor, but the other was a trick job in the window sill. Carl was kicking his psychology around when he had them built. Two safes in a house a person could expect, but rarely two in the same room. Anyone poking around couldn't miss the one behind the map, but it would take some inside dope to find the other. The dial was pretty badly beaten up and there were fresh scratches in the wood around the thing. I swung the door open, held my lighter in front of it and squinted around. The dust marked the outline of the box that had been there.

The cop had moved to the steps this time. He grinned and jerked his head at the house. "Not much to see."

"Who opened the safes?"

"The city boys brought Delaney in. He's the factory representative of the outfit who makes the safes. Good man. He could make a living working lofts."

"He's doing all right now," I said. I told him so-long and went back to the car. Lily was waiting, her face a pale glow behind the window.

I slid under the wheel, sat there fiddling with the gearshift letting the thought I had jell. Lily put her hand on my arm, held it still and waited. "I wonder if Pat found it," I muttered.

"What?"

"Michael Friday stooled on her brother. She went back home and found something else but this time she was afraid to give it to the police."

"Mike . . ."

"Let me talk, kid. You don't have to listen. I'm just getting it in order. There was trouble in the outfit. Carl was expecting to take over somehow. In that outfit you don't work your way up. Carl was expecting to move up a slot so somebody else had to go. That boy knew what he was doing. He spent some time getting something on the one he was after and was going to smear him with it."

I put it through my mind again, nodded, and said, "Carl was close enough to start the thing going so the other one knew about it. He went after what Carl had and found it gone. By that time the cops were having a field day with the labor department of the organization so he had a good idea who was responsible. He must have tailed her. He knew she had it and what she was going to do with it so he nailed her."

"But . . . who, Mike? Who?"

My teeth came apart in the kind of a smile nobody seemed to like. I was feeling good all over because I had my finger on it now and I wasn't letting go. "Friend Billy," I said. "Billy Mist. Now he sits quiet and enjoys his supper. Someplace he's got a dame on the hook and enjoying life because whatever it was Carl had isn't any more. Billy's free as a bird but he hasn't got two million in the bush to play with. He's got an ace in the hole with Velda in case the two million shows up and a deuce he can discard anytime if it doesn't. The greasy little punk is sitting pretty where he can't be touched."

The laugh started out of my chest and ripped through my throat. It was the biggest joke I ever laughed at because the whole play was made to block me out and I wasn't being mousetrapped. I was going back a couple of hours to the kitchen and what Lily had said and back even further to a note left in my office. Then, so I wouldn't forget how I felt right there at the beginning when I wanted to kill something with my hands, I went back to Berga and the way she had looked coming out of that gas station.

I kicked the engine over, pulled around the squad car and pointed the hood toward the bright eyes of Manhattan. I stayed with the lights watching the streets click by, cut over a few blocks to the building with the efficient look and antiseptic smell and pulled in behind the city hearse unloading a double cargo.

It was a little after one but you could still find dead people around.

The attendant in the morgue called me into his office and wanted to know if I wanted coffee. I shook my head. "It takes the smell away," he said. "What can I do for you?"

"You had a body here. Girl named Berga Torn."

"Still have it."

"Slated for autopsy?"

"Nope. At least I haven't heard about it. They don't usually in those cases."

"There will be one in this case. Can I use the phone?"

"Go ahead."

I picked it up and dialed headquarters. Pat wasn't around so I tried his apartment. He wasn't there, either. I buzzed a few of the places he spent time in but they hadn't seen him. I looked at my watch and the hand had spun another quarter. I swore at the phone and at myself and double cursed the red tape if I had to go through channels. I was thinking so hard I wasn't really thinking at all and while I was in the middle of it the door of the office opened and the little guy with the pot belly came in, dropped his bag on the floor and said, "Damn it, Charlie, why can't people wait until morning to die?"

I said, "Hi, doc," and the coroner gave me a surprised glance that wasn't any too pleased.

"Hello, Hammer, what are you doing here? Should I add 'again'?"

"Yeah, add it, doc. I always seem to come home, don't I?"

"I'd like it better if you stayed out of my sight."

He went to go past me. I grabbed his arm, turned him around and looked at a guy with a safe but disgusting job. He went up on his toes, tried to pull his arm away, but I held on. "Listen, doc. You and I can play games some other time. Right now I need you for a job that can't wait. I have to chop corners and it has to be quick."

"Let go of me!"

I let go of him. "Maybe you like to see those bodies stretched out in the gutter."

He turned around slowly. "What are you talking about?"

"Suppose you had a chance to do something except listen for a heartbeat that isn't there for a change. Supposing you had it in your hand to kick a few killers right into the chair. Supposing you're the guy who stands between a few more people living or dying in the next few hours . . . how would you pitch it, doc?"

The puzzle twisted his nose into a ridge of wrinkles. "See here . . . you're talking like . . ."

"I'm talking plain. I've been trying to get some official backing for what I have in mind but nobody's home. Even then it might take up time we can't spare. That chance I was talking about is in your hand, doc."

"But . . ."

"I need a stomach autopsy on a corpse. Now. Can do?"

"I think you're serious," he said in a flat tone.

"You'll never know how serious. There may be trouble later. Trouble isn't as bad as somebody having to die."

I could see the protest coming out of the attendant. It started but never got there. The coroner squared his shoulders, let a little of the excitement that was in my voice trickle into his eyes and he nodded.

"Berga Torn," I told the attendant. "Let's go see her."

He did it the fast, easy way you do when you cut corners. He did it right there in the carrier she lay on and the light overhead winked on the steel in his hand. I didn't get past the first glimpse because fire does horrible things to a person and it was nicer to remember Berga in the headlights of the car.

I could hear him, though.

I could even tell when he found it.

He did me the favor of cleaning it before he handed it to me and I stood there looking at the dull glitter of the brass key wondering where the lock to it was. The coroner said, "Well?"

"Thanks."

"I don't mean that."

"I know . . . only where it goes nobody knows. I thought it would be something else."

He sensed the disappointment and held out his hand. I dropped the key in it and he held it up to the light, turning it over to see both sides. For a minute he concentrated on one side, held it closer to the bulb, then nodded for me to follow him across the room. From a closet he pulled out a bottle of some acrid liquid, poured it into a shallow glass container, then dropped the key in. He let it stay there about twenty seconds before dipping it out with a glass rod. This time the dullness was gone. It was a gleaming thing with a new look and no coating to dull the details. This time when he held it in the light you could see *City Athletic Club, 529* scratched into the surface and I squeezed his arm so hard he winced through his grin.

I said, "Listen, get on the phone out there and find Captain Chambers. Tell him I found what we were looking for and I'm going after it. I'm not going to take any chances on this getting away so he can hop up to my office for a print of this thing."

"He doesn't know?"

"Uh-uh. I'm afraid somebody else might find out the same way I did. I'll call you back to see how you made out. If there's any trouble about . . . back there . . . Chambers'll clear things. Someday I'll let you know just how much of a boost up you gave the department."

The excitement in his eyes sparkled brighter and he was holding his jaw like a guy who's just done the impossible. The morgue attendant was on his way over for an explanation and apparently he wanted it in writing. He tried to stop me for some talk on the way out but I was in too much of a rush.

Lily knew I had it when I came bouncing down the stairs, opened the door for me and said, "Mike?"

"I know almost all the answers now, chicken." I held up the key. "Here's the big baby. Look at it, a chunk of metal people have died for and all this time it was in the stomach of a girl who was ready to do anything to beat them out of it. The key to the deal. For the first time in my life a real one. I know who had it and what's behind the door it opens."

As if the words I had said were a formula that split open Valhalla to let a pack of vicious, false gods spill through, a jagged streak of lightning cut across the sky with the thunder rolling in its wake. The first crashing wave of it was so sudden Lily tightened against it, her eyes closed tight.

I said, "Relax."

"I . . . can't, Mike. I hate thunderstorms."

You could feel the dampness in the air, the fresh coolness of the new wind. She shuddered again and turned up the little collar of her jacket around her neck. "Close the window, Mike."

I rolled it up, got the heap going and turned into traffic heading east. The voice of the city was starting to go quiet now. The last few figures on the streets were starting to run for cover and the cabs picked up their aimless cruising.

The first big drops of rain splattered on the hood and brought the scum flooding down the windshield. I started the wipers, but still had to hunch forward over the wheel to see where I was going.

I could feel time going by. The race of the minutes. They never went any faster or any slower, but they always beat you. I turned south on Ninth Avenue, staying in tempo with the lights until I reached the gray-brick building with the small neon sign that read CITY ATHLETIC CLUB.

I cut the engine in front of the door and went to get out. Lily said, "Mike, will you be long?"

"Couple of minutes." Her face seemed to be all pinched up.

"What's the matter, kid?"

"Cold, I guess."

I pulled the blanket from the seat in the back and draped it over her shoulders. "You're catching something sure as hell. Keep it around you. I'll be right back."

She shivered and nodded, holding the edges of the blanket together under her chin.

The guy at the reception desk was a sleepy-eyed tall guy who sat there hating everybody who bothered him. He watched me cross the hall and didn't make any polite sounds until I got to him.

He asked one question. "You a member?"

"No, but . . ."

"Then the place is closed. Scram."

I pulled a fin out of my wallet and laid it on the desk.

He said, "Scram."

I took it back, stuffed it away and leaned across the chair and belted him right on his back. I picked him up by his skinny arms and popped him a little one in the gut before I threw him back in his chair again. "The next time be nice," I said. I held out the key and he looked at it with eyes that were wide awake now.

"You bastard."

"Shut up. What's the key for?"

"Locker room."

"See who has 529."

He curled his lip at me, ran his hand across his stomach under his belt and pulled a ledger out of the desk drawer. "Raymond. Ten-year membership."

"Let's go."

"You're nuts. I can't leave the desk. I . . ."

"Let's go."

"Lousy coppers," I heard him say. I grinned behind his back and followed him down the stairs. There was a sticky dampness in the air, an acrid smell of disinfectant. We passed a steam room and the entrance to the pool, then turned into the alcove that held the lockers.

They were tall affairs with hasps that allowed you to install your own lock. Raymondo had slapped on a beauty. It was an oversized brass padlock with a snap so big it barely passed through the hasp. I stuck the key in, turned it and the lock came apart.

Death, crime and corruption was lying on the floor in two metal containers the size of lunch pails. The seams were welded shut and the units painted a deep green. Attached to each was the cutest little rig you ever saw, a small CO_2 bottle with a heavy rubber ball attached to the nozzle. The rubber was rotted in the folds and the hose connection had cracked dry, but it didn't spoil the picture any. All you had to do was toss the unit out a porthole, the bottle stopper opened after a time interval and the stuff floated to the top where the rubber ball buoyed it until it was picked up.

The answer to the *Cedric* was there too, a short story composed of sales slips stapled together, a yarn that said Raymondo had taken good care of his investment and was on hand to pick up the junk when they stripped the ship. There was one special item marked *"wall ventilators — 12.50 ea. 25.00."*

I squatted down to pull them out and the guy down the end came away from the wall showing too much curiosity. The stuff had to be dumped someplace but I couldn't be carrying it to the dumping ground. Pat had to see it, the Washington boys would want a look at it. I couldn't take any kind of a chance at all on losing it. Not now.

So I shut the door and closed the lock through the hasp. It had been there a lot of years . . . a few more hours wouldn't hurt it any. But now I had something I could talk a trade with. I could describe the stuff so they'd be sure and it would be my way all the way.

The guy followed me back upstairs and got behind his desk again. He was snottier looking than ever but when I stood close the artificial toughness faded into blankness and he had to lick his lips.

I said, "Remember my face, buddy. Take a good

look and keep it in your mind. If anybody who isn't a cop comes in here wanting to know about that locker and you kick through with the information I'm going to break your face into a dozen pieces. No matter what they do I'll do worse, so keep your trap shut." I turned to go, stopped a second and looked back over my shoulder. "The next time be polite. You could have made dough on the deal."

My watch read five minutes to three. Time, time, time. The rain was a solid sheet blasting the sidewalks and spraying back into the air again. I yelled for Lily to open the door, made a dash for it and slid aboard. She trembled under the gust of cold air that got in with me, her face set tighter than it was before.

I reached over and put my arm around her shoulders. She was pulled tight as a drumhead, a muscular stiffness that made her whole body almost immobile. "Cripes, Lily, I got to get you to a doctor."

"No . . . just get me where it's warm, Mike."

"I haven't got much sense."

She forced a smile. "I . . . really don't mind . . . as long as you . . ."

"No more chasing around, kid. I found it. I can take you back now."

There was a catch in the sob that came out of her. Her eyes glistened and the smile didn't have to be forced.

I sat there looking into the rain, pulling on a Lucky while I figured it out. I said, "You'll go back to my apartment, kid. Dry off and sit tight."

"Alone?"

"Don't worry about it. There are cops stationed around the building. I'll tip them to keep the place well covered. We have to move fast now and I can't waste time. I have a key to a couple of million bucks in my pocket and I can't put all my eggs in one basket. I'm getting a duplicate of that key made and you're hanging on to it until Captain Chambers picks it up. I don't want you to move out of that place until I get back and don't pull a stunt like you did before. Let's go, I still have a fast stop to make that won't take more than five minutes."

That was all it did take. My friend turned out the key while he swore at the world for getting him out of bed so I left him to buy a good night in a gin mill for his trouble.

We reached my block at a quarter to four with the rain still lashing at the car in frenzied bursts. There was a patrol wagon at each end and two plain-clothes men were standing in the doorway. When they saw us they looked so mad they could bust and one spit disgustedly and shook his head.

I didn't give them a chance to ask questions. "Sorry you were standing guard over a hole, friend. One of those things. We got this business breaking over our heads and I can't go explaining every move I make. I've been putting in calls all over the lot for Pat Chambers and if one of you guys feels like expediting things you'll get on the line too."

I pointed to Lily. "This is Lily Carver. They're after her as bad as they are me. She's got a message for Pat that can't wait and if anything happens to her between now and when he sees her he'll have your hides. One of you better take her up and stick outside in the hall."

"Johnston'll go."

"Good. You'll call around for Pat."

"We'll locate the captain somehow."

I got Lily inside, saw her through the front door with the cop beside her and felt the load go lighter.

"You got something, Hammer?" The cop was watching me closely.

"Yeah. It's almost over."

His grunt was a sarcastic denial. "You know better, buddy. It never ends. This thing is stretched all over the states. Wait till you see the morning papers."

"Good?"

"Lovely. The voters'll go nuts when they see the score. This town is going to see a reform cleanup like it never happened before. We had to book four of our own boys this evening." His hand turned into a fist. "They were playing along with them."

"The little guys," I said. "They pay through the nose. The wheels keep rolling right along. They string the dead out and walk over them. The little guy pays the price."

"We got wheels too. Evello's dead."

"Yeah," I said.

"How far did they get with his step-sister?"

"As far as here, buddy. People are thinking about that."

I looked across the lobby at him. "They would. They'll try to put the finger anyplace."

Michael Friday and her wet, lovely mouth. The mouth that never did get close enough, really close. Michael Friday with the ready smile and the laugh in her walk, Michael Friday who got tired of the dirt herself and put herself on my side of the fence. Coming to me with the thing I wanted even more than the stuff in the locker. She should have known. Damn it, those things had been happening under her nose. She should have known the kind of people she was messing around with. They're fast and smart and know the angles and they're ready to follow through. She should have thought it out and got herself a cordon of cops instead of cutting loose herself to get the stuff to me. Maybe she knew they'd be after her. Maybe she thought she was as smart as they were. Berga thought those things too.

Lovely Michael Friday. She steps outside and they have her. She could have been standing right where I was that minute. The door behind her locks shut. There's only one person outside and that's the one she's afraid of. Maybe she knew she only had a minute more to live and her insides must have been tumbling around loose.

Like Berga. But Berga did something in that minute.

I got that creepy feeling again, an indescribably tingling sensation that burned up my spine and touched my brain with thoughts that seemed improbable. I looked down at my feet, my teeth shut tight, squinting at the floor. The cop's breathing seemed the loudest thing in the room, even drowning out the thunder and the rain outside. I walked to the mailbox and opened it with my key.

Michael had thought too. She had left an empty envelope in there telling me exactly what she meant. It didn't have my name on it, but I read the message. It said, "William Mist," but it was enough.

It was more than enough. It was something else. The gimmick I was looking for, the one I knew I had come across someplace else but I couldn't put my finger on. But for a little while it was enough.

I crumpled the thing up into a little ball and dropped it. I could feel the hate welling up in me until I couldn't stand it any more. My head was filled with a crazy overture of sound that beat and beat and beat.

I ran out of the place. I left the cop standing there and ran out. I forgot everything I was doing except for one thing when I got in the car. Light, traffic? Hell, nothing mattered. There was only one thing. I was going to see that greaseball die between my fingers and he was going to talk before he did. The car screamed at the corners, the tail end whipping around violently. I could smell the rubber and brake lining and hear the whining protest of the engine and occasionally the hoarse curses that followed my path. The stops were all out this time and nothing else counted.

When I reached the apartment building I didn't push any bells to be let in. I kicked out a pane of glass on the inside door, reached through the hole and turned the knob. I went up the stairs to the same spot I had been before and this time I did hit the bell.

Billy Mist was expecting somebody, all right, but it wasn't me. He was all dressed except for his jacket and he had a gun slung in a harness under his shoulder. I rammed the door so hard it kicked him back in the room and while he was reaching for his rod I smashed his nose into a mess of bloody tissue. He made a second try while he was on the floor and this time I kicked the gun out of his hand under the table and picked him up to go over him good. I held him out where I wanted him and put one into his ribs that brought a scream choking up his throat and had the next one ready when Billy Mist died.

I didn't want to believe it. I wanted him alive so bad I shook him like a rag doll and when the mouth lolled open under those blank eyes I threw him away from me into the door and his head and shoulders slammed it shut. His broken face leered at me from the carpet, the eyes seeing nothing. They were filmy already. I let it go then. I let that raspy yell out of me and began to break things until I was out of breath.

But Billy still leered.

Billy Mist, who knew where Velda was. Billy Mist who was going to talk before he died. Billy

Mist who was going to give me the pleasure of killing him slowly.

It was thinking of Velda that smoothed it. My hands stopped shaking and my mind started thinking again. I looked around the mess I had made of the place, avoiding the eyes on the floor.

Billy had been packing. He had been five minutes away from being killed and he was taking a quick-acting powder. The one suitcase had a week's supply of clothes in it but he could afford to buy more when he got there because the rest of the space was taken up by packets of new bills.

I was picking the stuff apart when I heard them at the door. They weren't cops. Not these boys. They wanted in because I was there and nothing was stopping them.

How long ago was it that I asked Berga how stupid could she get?

Now I was the one. Sammy had told me. They were waiting for me. Not in squad cars on the corner of my block. Now for the Ford because by now they'd have figured the switch. So I go busting loose with the pack on my back and now I was up the tree.

Shoulders slammed into the door and a vertical crack showed in it. I walked to the overturned chair, picked up Billy's rod and kicked the safety off. They were a little stupid too. They knew I was traveling clean but forgot Billy would be loaded. I pumped five fast ones through the wood belly-high and the screams outside made a deafening cacophony that brought more screams from others in the building.

The curses and screams didn't stop the others. The door cracked again, started to buckle and I turned and ran into the bathroom. There was a barrel bolt on the door made for decency purposes only and wouldn't hold anything longer than a minute or two. I slid it in place, took my time about opening the bathroom window and sighting along the ledge outside.

I got my feet on the sill, started to go through when my arm swept the bottles from the shelf. Dozens of bottles. A sick man's paradise and Billy had been a very sick man after all. There was one left my arm didn't touch and I picked it up. I stared at it, swore lightly and dropped it in my pocket.

The door inside let loose. There was more letting loose too. Shots and shrieks that didn't belong there and I crawled through the window before I could find out why. I felt along the ledge with my toes, leaning forward at an angle with my hands resting on the building on the other side of the airway. I made the end where the building joined, found handholds on the other sills and went up.

For a change I was glad of the rain. It covered the noises I made, washed clean places for my fingers and toes and when I reached the roof bathed me in its coolness. I lay there on the graveled top breathing the fire out of my lungs, barely conscious of the fury going on in the streets. When I could make it I got across the building, got on the fire escape and crawled down.

Somebody in a dark window was screaming her lungs out telling the world where I was. Shouts answered her from someplace else and two shots whined off into the night. They never found me. I hit the yard and got out of there. Sirens were converging on the place and a hundred yards off the rapid belch of a tommy gun spit a skinful of sudden destruction into the airway.

I laughed my fool head off while I stood there on the sidewalk and felt good about it. In a way it paid to be stupid as long as you overdid it. I was too stupid to figure the boys planted around my apartment would follow me and too stupid to remember there were the Washington boys who would run behind them. It must have made a pretty picture when they joined forces. It was something that had to come. The Mafia wasn't a gang, it was a government. And governments have armies and armies fight.

The trouble was that while the war raged the leader got away and had time to cover his tracks. I pulled the bottle out of my pocket, looked at it and threw it away.

Not this leader. He wasn't going anywhere except a hole in the ground.

Chapter Thirteen

The office was dark. Water leaked through the hole I had made in the glass and the pieces winked back at me. Nobody at the desk. No beautiful smile, challenging eyes. I knew where to look and pulled the file out. I held a match to it and the pieces clicked in place. I put the card back and went through the rooms.

Off the inner office a door led to stairs that ran up, thickly carpeted stairs that didn't betray the passage of a person. There was another door at the top and an apartment off it. I kicked my shoes off, laid the change in my pocket on the floor and walked away from the one that showed the light.

There was only one room that was locked, but those kind of locks never gave me any trouble at all. I stepped inside, eased the door shut and flicked my lighter.

She was laced into an easy chair with a strait jacket, her legs tied down. A strip of adhesive tape across her mouth and around it were red marks where other tapes had been ripped off to feed her or hear what she had to say. There was a sallowness about her face, a fearful, shrunken look, but the eyes were alive. They couldn't see me behind the lighter, but they cursed me just the same.

I said, "Hello, Velda," and the cursing stopped. The eyes didn't believe until I moved the lighter and the tears wiped out her vision. I took the ropes off, unlaced the jacket and lifted her up easily. The hurt sounds she wanted to make but couldn't came out in the convulsions of her body. She pressed against me, the tears wetting my face. I squeezed her, ran my hands across her back while I whispered things to her and told her not to be afraid any more. I found her mouth and tasted her, deeply, loving the way she held me and the things she said without really saying anything.

When I could I said, "You all right?"

"I was going to die tonight."

"Somebody'll take your place."

"Now?"

"You won't be here to see it." I found the key in my pocket and pressed it in her hand. I gave her my wallet to go with it and pulled her to the door. "Take a cab and find yourself a cop. Find Pat if you can. There's an address on that key. Go hold what's in the locker it opens. Can you do that much?"

"Can't I . . ."

"I said get a cop. The bastards know everything there is to know. We can't lose any time at all . . . and most of all I can't lose you at all. Tomorrow we'll talk."

"Tomorrow, Mike."

"It's crazy this way. Everything's crazy. I find

you and I'm sending you off again. Damn it, move before I don't let you go."

"Tomorrow, Mike," she said and reached for me again. She wasn't tired now, she was brand-new again. She was a woman I was never going to let go again ever. She didn't know it yet, but tomorrow there would be more than talk. I wanted her since I had first seen her. Tomorrow I'd get her. The way she wanted it. Tomorrow she was going to belong to me all the way.

"Say it, Mike."

"I love you, kitten. I love you more than I've ever thought I could love anything."

"I love you too, Mike." I could feel her grin. "Tomorrow."

I nodded and opened the door. I waited until she had gone down the steps and this time walked the other way. To where the light showed.

I pushed it open, leaned against the sill and when the gray-haired man writing at the table across the room spun around I said, "Doctor Soberin, I presume."

It caught him so far off base I had time to get halfway across to him before he dipped his hand in the drawer and I had his wrist before he could get the thing leveled. I let him keep the gun in his hand so I could bend it back and hear his fingers break and when he tried to yell I bottled the sound up by smashing my elbow into his mouth. The shattered teeth tore my arm and his mouth became a great hole welling blood. His fingers were broken stubs sticking at odd angles. I shoved him away from me, slashed the butt end of the rod across the side of his head and watched him drop into his chair.

"I got me a wheel," I said. "The boy at the top."

Dr. Soberin opened his mouth to speak and I shook my head.

"You're dead, mister. Starting from now you're dead. It took me a long time. It didn't really have to." I let out a dry laugh at myself. "I'm getting too old for the game. I'm not as fast as I used to be. One time I would have had it made as soon as I rolled it around a little bit.

"The gimmick, doc, there's always that damned gimmick. The kind you can't kick out of sight. This time the gimmick was on the bottom of that card your secretary made out on Berga Torn. She asked who sent her and she said William Mist. She signed the card, too. You pulled a cutie on that one. You couldn't afford to let a respectable dame know your business, and you knew she wouldn't put her name on a switch. You knew there might be an investigation and didn't want any suspicious erasures on the card so you simply dug up a name that you could type over Mist to make the letters fit. Wieton comes out pretty well. Unless you looked hard you'd never pick it up."

He had gone a deathly pale. His hand was up to his mouth trying to stop the blood. It was sickening him and he retched. All that came up was more blood. The hand with the broken fingers looked unreal on the end of his arm. Unreal and painful.

"You took a lot of trouble to get the information Berga had under her hat. A lot of clever thinking went into that deal at the sanitarium. You had it rigged pretty nicely, even to a spot where she could be worked over without anybody getting wise. Sorry I spoiled your plans. You shouldn't have wrecked my heap."

Something childish crept into his face. "You . . . got . . . another one."

"I'll keep it too. I didn't go for the booby trap, doc. That was kid stuff."

If his face screwed up any tighter he was going to cry. He sat there moaning softly, the complete uncertainty of it all making him rock in his chair.

I said, "This time I do it your way. I was the only one you were ever afraid of because I was like the men you give orders to. I'm not going to talk to you. Later I'll go over the details. Later I'll give my explanations and excuses to the police. Later I'll get raked over the coals for what I'm going to do now, but what the hell, doc. Like I said, I'm getting old in the game. I don't care any more."

He was quiet in his chair. The quiet that terror brings and for once he was knowing the hand of terror himself.

I said, "Doc . . ." and he looked at me. No, not me, the gun. The big hole in the end of the gun.

And while he was looking I let him see what

279

came out of the gun.

Doctor Soberin only had one eye left.

I stepped across the body and picked up the phone. I called headquarters and tried to get Pat. He was still out. I had the call transferred to another department and the man I wanted said hello. I asked him for the identification on a dead blonde and he told me to wait.

A minute later he picked up the phone. "Think I got it. Death by drowning. Age, about . . ."

"Skip the details. Just the name."

"Sure, Lily Carver. Prints just came in from Washington. She had 'em taken while she worked at a war plant."

I said thanks, held the button down on the phone, let it go and when I heard the dial tone started working on my home number.

She said, "Don't bother, Mike. I'm right here."

And she was.

Beautiful Lily with hair as white as snow. Her mouth a scarlet curve that smiled. Differently, now, but still smiling. Her body a tight bundle of lush curves that swelled and moved under a light white terrycloth robe. Lovely Lily who brought the sharpness of an alcohol bath in with her so that it wet her robe until there was nothing there, no hill or valley, no shadow that didn't come out.

Gorgeous Lily with my .45 in her hand from where she had found it on the dresser.

"You forgot about me, Mike."

"I almost did, didn't I."

There was cold hate coming into her eyes now. Hate that grew as she looked again at the one eye in the body beside the table. "You shouldn't have done that, Mike."

"No?"

"He was the only one who knew about me." The smile left her mouth. "I loved him. He knew about me and didn't care. I loved him, you crumb you!" The words hissed out of her teeth.

I looked at her the way I did when she first held a gun on me. "Sure. You loved him so much you killed Lily Carver and took her place. You loved him so much you made sure there were no slips in his plan. You loved him so much you set Berga Torn up for the kill and damn near made sure Velda died. You loved him so much you never saw that all he loved was power and money and you were only something he could use.

"You fitted right into the racket. You were lucky once and smart the rest of the time. You reached Al after Velda left but you had time to catch up with her. By the way, did you ever find out why Al died? He was giving friend Billy Mist the needle. Billy knew what had happened when you called him down to tell him his girl friend wasn't what she was cracked up to be. With Billy that didn't go and he carved up his playmate. Nice people to have around."

"Shut up."

"Shut up hell. You stuck with me all the way. You ducked out because you thought the boys had me once, then came back when you found out I

281

propped them up against a dead-end sign. You passed the word right under my nose and had Billy packing to blow town. What a deal that was. I even showed you how to get out of my apartment without a tail picking you up. That's why you're here now. So what was supposed to happen? You go back to your real identity? Nuts. You're part of it and you'll die with it. You played me for a sucker up and down Broadway but it's over. This isn't the first time you've pointed a rod at me, sugar. The last time was a game, but I didn't know it. I'm still going to take it away from you. What kind of a guy do you think I am anyway?"

Her face changed as if I had slapped her. For an instant the strangeness was back again. "You're a deadly man, Mike."

Then I saw it in her face and she was faster than I was. The rod belched flame and the slug tore into my side and spun me around. There was a crazy spinning sensation, a feeling of tumbling end over end through space, an urge to vomit, but no strength left to vomit with.

My eyes cleared and I pushed myself up on an elbow. There was a loose, empty feeling in my joints. The end was right there ahead of me and nothing I could do about it.

Lily smiled again, the end of the .45 drifting down to my stomach. She laughed at me, knowing I could raise myself to reach for it. My mouth was dry. I wanted a cigarette. It was all I could think about. It was something a guy about to die always got. My fingers found the deck of Luckies, fumbled one loose and got it into my mouth. I could barely feel it lying there on my lips.

"You shouldn't have killed him," Lily said again.

I reached for the lighter. It wasn't going to be long now. I could feel things start to loosen up. My mind was having trouble hearing her. One more shot. It would be quick.

"Mike . . ."

I got my eyes open. She was a strong, pungent smell. Very strong. Still lovely though.

"I thought I almost loved you once. More than . . . him. But I didn't Mike. He would take me like I was. He was the one who gave me life, at least, after . . . it happened. He was the doctor. I was the patient. I loved him. You would have been disgusted with me. I can see your eyes now, Mike. They would have been revolted.

"He was deadly too, Mike . . . but not like you. You're even worse. You're the deadly one, but you would have been revolted. Look at me, Mike. How would you like to kiss me now? You wanted to before. Would you like to now? I wanted you to . . . you know that, don't you? I was afraid to even let you touch me. You wanted to kiss me . . . so kiss me."

Her fingers slipped through the belt of the robe, opened it. Her hands parted it slowly . . . until I could see what she was really like. I wanted to vomit worse than before. I wanted to let my guts come up and felt my belly retching.

She was a horrible caricature of a human! There was no skin, just a disgusting mass of twisted, puckered flesh from her knees to her neck making a picture of gruesome freakishness that made you want to shut your eyes against it.

The cigarette almost fell out of my mouth. The lighter shook in my hand, but I got it open.

"Fire did it, Mike. Do you think I'm pretty now?"

She langhed and I heard the insanity in it. The gun pressed into my belt as she kneeled forward, bringing the revulsion with her. "You're going to die now . . . but first you can do it. Deadly . . . deadly . . . kiss me."

The smile never left her mouth and before it was on me I thumbed the lighter and in the moment of time before the scream blossoms into the wild cry of terror she was a mass of flame tumbling on the floor with the blue flames of alcohol turning the white of her hair into black char and her body convulsing under the agony of it. The flames were teeth that ate, ripping and tearing, into scars of other flames and her voice the shrill sound of death on the loose.

I looked, looked away. The door was closed and maybe I had enough left to make it.